Ex-mas

12-09

OTHER BOOKS BY KATE BRIAN

LUCKY T

THE PRINCESS & THE PAUPER

THE V CLUB

MEGAN MEADE'S GUIDE TO THE McGOWAN BOYS

SWEET 16

FAKE BOYFRIEND

Ex-mas

BY

KATE BRIAN

SIMON & SCHUSTER BFYR

New York   London   Toronto   Sydney

Ex-mas

1

NORTH VALLEY HIGH SCHOOL
LOS ANGELES
DECEMBER 22
11:43 A.M.

Mr. Geary had to be kidding.

It was literally *moments* before the last bell was supposed to ring on the last half-day of classes—three seconds to Christmas break and the holidays and *freedom*—and the earth science teacher was handing out homework with every indication that he expected people to be paying attention. Had he finally lost it?

"He must be insane," Lila Beckwith muttered to her lab partner, Denny. She took the handout with a heavy sigh and scanned the first page, picking out the words *global warming* and *polar ice caps* before stuffing the article into her bag. Winter break was about to start and she had far more pressing things to attend to. For example, the biggest party of the year. Which she happened to be throwing. Tonight.

Assuming earth science ever ended.

RINNNGGGGG!

Finally!

Lila leaped from her seat and raced for the door, getting caught up in the swell of excited kids streaming down the hallway. The lacrosse guys jostled one another outside the classroom. A pack of drama geeks linked arms and sang "Rockin' Around the Christmas Tree" in four-part harmony as they headed past the main office. Such was Lila's sudden rush of vacation-induced holiday spirit that for once she didn't even find them annoying.

The sea of laughing, happy teenagers swept through the halls and out the front door, delivering Lila into a typically perfect Southern California day. The sky was blue and flawless, palm trees rustled in the slight breeze, and the sun was warm on her face. Off to the south, the Santa Monica Mountains rose in the distance, marking the barrier between the San Fernando Valley and the city of Los Angeles. The front steps of North Valley High were divided too: Seniors lounged around the upper steps in their assorted social groups, juniors took over the flat landing below them, and underclassmen occupied the lowest steps, closest to the parking lot. Lila pushed her dark hair over her shoulder with a smile. Every single one of them wanted to go to her party.

"I hope you're ready for tonight!" Lila's best friend, Carly, called from her usual place at the top of the wide steps, surrounded by a cluster of girls. She was blond and sunny—the perfect foil to Lila's dark brunette looks. Lila liked to think of them as yin and yang, or Serena and Blair. Together, they were the leaders of the most popular group of girls in the senior class, and thus the entirety of North Valley High.

"You know it," Lila said with a grin, easing her way to the place reserved for her at Carly's side. Yoon Lee and Rebecca Gans, two inseparable seniors, parted ways to make room, and Melinda Dennis, an enterprising, wide-eyed sophomore, practically polished the railing for her to lean against. Lila eased between the girls, happy to be at the center of their group. She'd worked hard to get there, after all. If she wished that it all came as effortlessly to her as it did to carefree, beautiful, and beloved Carly, well, she kept that to herself.

"I can't believe my parents are *finally* going out of town," Lila said with a dramatic eye roll. The other girls pressed closer. Jeannine Fargo looked like she was about to keel over from the excitement—or maybe she'd eaten nothing but carrots again today. "They seriously never go anywhere. I have no idea what act of God has reversed their entire lifestyle and personal history for this weekend, but who am I to look a gift horse in the mouth?"

"Is E coming down?" Carly asked, flashing her famous, infectious grin. It had the same warming effect on everyone, including Lila. How could you not smile back?

"Absolutely," Lila said. "He wouldn't miss it." *E* was Erik, Carly's older brother and Lila's boyfriend. They'd been dating for almost three years, and he was driving down from Stanford tonight, where he was a freshman. They'd barely seen each other all fall—he needed to get settled at school, and her parents insisted she focus on her classes and SATs—but with any luck, this would be the longest they'd ever be apart. Next year at this time, she hoped to be at Stanford alongside him. It had been her dream school since forever, and the fact that Erik went there was like an amazing two-for-one sale at Fred Segal.

"You guys are so lucky," Melinda gushed, on cue.

Lila was not about to tell Melinda, now or ever, that luck had nothing to do with how her life had turned out. People didn't just *end up* best friends with Carly Hollander, much less dating Erik, who was a year ahead of them and voted both Most Attractive and Most Likely to Succeed in last year's yearbook superlatives. Lila had taken advantage of a few key opportunities—like Carly's big falling-out with her former best friend, Jeannine—and she'd done it without acting all creepy and gushy like Melinda, thank you very much.

"I heard people are driving up from the O.C. to come tonight," Rebecca broke in, railroading the conversation like she always did. "Michelle Reynolds said she read about it on her cousin's Twitter, and he lives all the way down in San Juan Capistrano. It's going to be legendary."

Lila leaned back as the conversation swelled up around her, listening with pleasure as everyone debated the rumors they'd heard about the party she hadn't even thrown yet. Tonight was going to rock, and when it did, it would cement her reputation forevermore. No more waiting for everyone to wake up one day and realize that she was a former nobody. No more *Erik Hollander's girlfriend* or *Carly Hollander's best friend*. Oh, no. She would be Lila Beckwith, all on her own.

She could hardly wait.

Her eyes fell on a single solitary figure heading toward the parking lot. He pushed his shaggy black hair off his forehead and hoisted his so-uncool-it-was-cool black canvas JanSport farther up on his back.

Beau Hodges. All alone. Of course.

Not that she felt sorry for him. Beau *chose* to be alone, just like he *chose* to embrace being a loser each and every day of his high school career. Witness his clothes: dirty hoodie over a ripped-up old concert T-shirt featuring some obscure band, jeans Lila was pretty sure he'd worn back in seventh grade, and his trademark *up yours, world* slouch, which called attention to his messy dark hair and his brooding, lazy blue eyes that were always, *always* filled with way too much attitude. He was everything enraging, wrapped up in one lean, hipsterish package.

It was hard to imagine that she had ever dated him.

But the facts were the facts, and anyway, it was ancient

history at this point. Beau was her ex-boyfriend, something very few people even remembered these days, given that Lila was, well, Lila and Beau was . . . busy being Beau. They had been together all through middle school and for most of ninth grade, up until Lila started hanging out with Carly and Beau had acted like Carly was the head recruiter for the local leper colony. His loss. He had gone on to his exciting career as a teenage nonentity, and Lila was dating Erik Hollander and about to throw the biggest party of the year.

Was there really any competition?

Her Nokia buzzed and she pulled it out of her distressed leather tote. *Erik* flashed on the screen. She held up a finger to her crew before answering, as if they hadn't already heard the distinctive, Erik-only ringtone: "Sugar" by Flo Rida.

"Tell me you're already on your way," she said, watching Beau get into his beat-up Ford Escort. He pulled off his faded gray hoodie and threw it in the backseat. Erik, thank God, would never be caught dead shuffling around in public looking like he'd slept in his clothes. "Or better yet, that you made it home early."

"Hey, babe," Erik replied. Lila loved his voice, so low and always sweet when he called her *babe*. She closed her eyes and pictured him: Erik was tall, with wide, football-strong shoulders and a confident swagger—a blond Californian god with the requisite surfer's body and the yummiest hazel eyes in the world. And he was all Lila's. It was like a dream, except for the part where it was completely and deliciously real.

"I can't wait to see you," Lila murmured.

"Me either," Erik replied, a little too quickly for comfort. "But babe—I'm not going to make it down tonight. I'm really sorry."

"What do you mean?" Lila's eyes popped open, her voice squeaking despite herself. *What do you mean you're not going to make it?* she wanted to scream. But she knew she couldn't lose it. Not in public. Not with everyone watching.

From her perch at the top steps, she could see the whole school was splayed out in front of her, in descending order of social importance. For a brief second, she wished she were down on the lowest steps, where she could have a private conversation without everybody listening. She wished she were in the parking lot, even. Invisible, like Beau.

But only for a brief second.

"One of my professors sprang this take-home final on us today, out of nowhere," Erik said with a heavy sigh. "I've already been at the library for three hours, and it doesn't look like I'll finish anytime soon. It has to be in by eight a.m. tomorrow, and that means there's just no way I can get it done and still make it to L.A. . . ." He sighed again, and she imagined him making that concerned frown, with his forehead wrinkled up and his mouth pulled down, the way he always did when he was upset about something. "I'm really sorry, Lila."

"Oh, no worries," Lila said, trying to sound understanding. Carly's eyebrows were raised in a question mark. "I completely understand."

"And I'll be home before Christmas, don't worry," Erik continued, his tone lighter now. "Just a couple more days, I promise."

"You just concentrate on your final," Lila said in her sweetest, best Supportive Girlfriend voice, "and I'll see you when I see you."

She deserved the freaking Girlfriend of the Year Award, she thought as she hit the button to end the call. Or an Oscar.

"Oh, no," Yoon said, with what sounded like *mostly* sincere supportiveness. "What happened to Erik?"

"Don't tell me he's too hungover for the drive," Carly said with a laugh.

Lila smiled breezily at her girls. "He got slammed with a surprise final," she said, shrugging her shoulders. The crisp Los Angeles air seemed to slice right through her plaid Alice + Olivia button-down. "You should have heard how bummed he was." She wrinkled up her nose and grinned at Carly. "Your brother is so cute!"

"I think I just threw up in my mouth," Carly replied, and everyone laughed. She reached over and linked her arm through Lila's.

Lila let herself lean on Carly, just a little bit. It wasn't like Erik was letting her down—he had exams. But her whole fantasy of cohosting a fabulous party with her perfect college boyfriend was crumbling faster than a stale Christmas cookie in January.

As her clique started moving toward the parking lot, Lila shook out her glossy, dark mane, forcing herself to regroup. Forget the pity party—she had a *real* party to plan. Her entire future depended on it.

The North Pole might be melting, but hell would freeze over before Lila Beckwith committed social suicide.

2

Lila read through her iCal to-do list on her laptop. There was still plenty to do before tonight: She had a full bar to set up, a dance-worthy playlist to compile, and mistletoe to hang all over the house (really, the only Christmas tradition that suited her). When it came to her party, she was completely ready to bring it.

Which would be a lot easier to do if her parents would just hurry up and leave the house already.

"Cooper, sweetie!" Lila's mother's voice rang out through all three stories of the Beckwith's craftsman-style house. "Can you please pick up your art project from the kitchen?"

Lila could hear her little brother's thudding footsteps as he came flying down the stairs.

"Lila," Mrs. Beckwith called from the kitchen. "You really

should see Cooper's drawing. I think we have a little Picasso on our hands!"

"He's very talented," Lila called back, even though she had not been quite as impressed with eight-year-old Cooper's construction paper scribbles as her mother appeared to be. Even if he *was* destined to be the next Picasso, Lila doubted that her mother, who collected novelty snow globes, was qualified to say so.

Lila sat in the family room adjacent to the kitchen, supposedly working on the family Christmas card on her iBook while secretly IMing her booze hookup about the night's delivery. The Christmas card had been her personal task since she was a kid and had begged for the honor, sending out one appalling drawing after another, which her parents apparently thought was cute. So cute that they still displayed the cards every year in the taupe-upholstered family room, from Thanksgiving through New Year's. The cringe-inducing scribbles were framed and hung at even three-inch intervals along the mantle.

"How's the card coming along?" her mother asked, appearing in the wide archway in front of her. Mrs. Beckwith had cornflower blue eyes and short, light brown hair that was neatly curled at her chin. She wore a string of pearls around her neck at all times.

Lila smiled innocently, minimizing the IM box just in case her mother had suddenly developed X-ray vision and could see through the laptop to the screen.

"Oh, you know." Lila shrugged. "It's coming." She felt guilty about lying for approximately a second. But then she reminded herself that her parents still refused to get Lila her own car—despite the fact that she was a *senior* and lived in *Los Angeles*, where there were nothing but vast distances between everything, often with *mountains*—and got over it. They claimed there might be a car for Lila's eighteenth birthday in January that she could take with her to college, and had been dangling the promise ever since she got her learner's permit. It was behind every threat they ever made: *Clean your room before you go out, or no car for you. Better impress us with those midterm grades, or forget that car.* And so on. But who knew if they'd even keep their word? The car could just be an elaborate scheme, something they'd read in a parenting book somewhere. *Discipline via positive motivation.* At this point, Lila wouldn't be surprised to discover it was as much an illusion as Santa Claus.

"One of these years I'd like to send the card out before New Year's Eve," Mrs. Beckwith added, with a pointed look at her daughter.

"You can't rush the creative process." Lila tried to ease her spine back against the plush cushions of the couch. *Relax,* she cautioned herself. *They're leaving. You can make it.* "Aren't you guys taking off soon?"

"We leave in half an hour," Mrs. Beckwith said, her thin pink lips in a slight frown. "Are you sure you're going to be okay with Cooper?" she asked. Her tone said, *Are you sure you're not going to burn down the house with our precious little eight-year-old inside?*

"Yes, Mom." Lila suppressed an eye roll. "You know, a lot of people actually *hire* seventeen-year-olds to watch their kids. And here I'm happy to do it for free," she added for a little guilt-inducing effect. Her parents had never left her alone with Cooper. This weekend was a first.

A long-awaited, much-anticipated, seriously overdue first.

"Have you packed?" Lila asked, enjoying the look of confusion that passed over her mother's face. Ultra-organized Mrs. Beckwith had showered the night before and packed days in advance, in sets of color-coordinated separates.

Her mother didn't answer the absurd question, and disappeared back into the kitchen. No doubt to supervise Cooper, even though he was *eight*—not *eight months*. Not that Lila's parents seemed to notice that distinction. They treated him like a baby, and like some chicken-and-egg paradox—*ta-da!*—he acted like a baby.

Cooper had been born early and with complications. Lila could remember what it was like back then, with her parents so freaked out about the surgery he'd needed. She'd been scared too. But eight years later, he was a happy, healthy, mischievous eight-year-old kid. And yet they *still* treated Cooper like he might break at any moment—all while acting like Lila was a breath away from becoming a juvenile delinquent. When the truth was, she had terrific grades (3.92 GPA, thank you very much), headed up the yearbook committee (how else would she ensure no one ever forgot her?), and played second doubles on the tennis team (sculpted calves? check). At the very least, she deserved to be left in charge of her own transportation. Was that really too much to ask?

She maximized the chat window and typed, THINK SOONER BETTER THAN L8R, OK? PARENTS LEAVING SOON AND THIS PARTY NEEDS 2 START ASAP!

Suddenly a grubby, marker-stained hand grabbed her from behind.

"Aaah!" Lila yelped.

"Made you flinch!" Cooper crowed in delight from the back of the couch. Little brat. At least he was over his Indian-burn phase. That had practically left scars.

Lila gave him her patented Death Glare and slapped her computer shut. "You are a troll," she told him icily.

"Mom said I could help you with the Christmas card," Cooper announced, his brown eyes lighting up as he danced on the carpet. Cooper was small for his age, with short, light brown hair, a frustratingly cherubic freckled face, and clothing permanently stained with markers, paint, cake batter, even (grr) Lila's Nars foundation—anything he could get his hands on or into. "I drew a picture of Santa! A good one! If I leave it out for him, do you think he'll like it?"

How Cooper had managed to survive all the way to the third grade with his belief in Santa intact was a mystery. MacKenzie Bolton had ruined the whole thing for Lila in kindergarten, bringing in a time-stamped photograph of the Boltons' dad leaving presents under the tree and even eating the sugar cookies left out for Santa. But Lila's parents found it adorable, and insisted that no one in the Beckwith house ruin Christmas for Cooper.

Because she knew her mother was listening, aka *monitoring* her, from the next room, Lila forced herself to respond nicely. "Nice one, Coop," she said, taking the supposed Picasso from his hands. The drawing was—surprise!—a glorified stick figure, sporting a fur-trimmed red hat. "But how do you know it looks like him? You fell asleep before you could take his picture last year, remember?"

"Everyone knows what Santa looks like, Lila," Cooper said matter-of-factly, like he couldn't believe Lila had said something so moronic. "He's more famous than the president!"

"You know this is Cooper's favorite time of year, Lila," her mother called from the other room. "You don't have to let him help you with your Christmas card, but maybe while we're away you can help him build one of those gingerbread houses he likes, or bake some Christmas cookies."

Cooper wriggled around in joy, a mess of freckles and suspiciously stained green sweatshirt and *boy* on the carpet in front of her. Now that the idea of gingerbread houses and cookies was implanted in his little brain, there would be no escaping it.

"But let's make sure Cooper doesn't eat too many cookies, or too much candy," Mrs. Beckwith continued from the adjacent kitchen. "We have to watch his carbohydrate count. Too many carbs can cause digestion problems."

"Don't worry, Mom." Lila tapped her fingertips on the sleek white top of her iBook. She made a mental note to give herself a manicure before people started showing up tonight. "I'll eat all the leftover carbs."

"As long as Cooper doesn't!" her mother singsonged. Lila's digestive system, presumably, could sort itself out.

Lila stared down at her ragged fingernails. Her parents' attitude certainly wasn't doing Cooper any favors. Lila knew, because she'd been almost as clueless about life at Cooper's age, and look what it had gotten her—years spent closely investigating extreme loserdom from the inside. She'd wandered through middle school with a selection of fuzzy ponytails on top of her head, Ugly Betty's fashion sense, and no idea how to make the right friends. She and Beau had been best friends growing up and had slid into boyfriend-girlfriend territory in the seventh grade, existing in a little cocoon of first kisses and music. Lila had had some Beau Hodges–induced fantasy about wanting to be a professional singer someday—the kind of professional singer, apparently, who didn't care about her appearance, content to look like a frizzy-haired Labradoodle.

It wasn't until high school that Lila woke up and smelled the Frédéric Fekkai smoothing cream. She'd had the extraordinarily good fortune of being falsely accused of cheating on a test in a freshman history class. The other suspected culprit? Carly Hollander. Since nothing could be proven and both girls denied it, they'd escaped the school's harsher disciplinary measures, but had been forced to serve two weeks of detention together.

Those had been the most educational two weeks of Lila's life. She had come out of those detentions with a coveted invitation to Carly's birthday party and a bone-deep determination to completely change her look and her life. Enough with Lila Beckwith, the starry-eyed loser who drifted around the fringes at North Valley High. It was time to grow up and stop hiding.

Lila had invited Beau to the party. But he'd acted like she was personally betraying him by wanting to hang out with "the zombies," as he called the popular kids—Carly Hollander being the Queen Zombie of their class. Their blowup had ended with Lila going to the party newly single—and *leaving* the party with Erik as her new boyfriend. Just like that, she'd grown up.

Something Cooper needed to do, stat.

"I really want cookies *and* a gingerbread house," the little monster was saying now, digging his Heely sneaker into the thick beige carpet. "Don't do that thing you do where you promise stuff because Mom's here and then don't do it. I hate that."

Lila braced herself, expecting her mother to come charging in from the kitchen in a righteous fury, outraged that precious Cooper might suffer so much as one second of disappointment at Lila's hands.

But somehow, it didn't happen. A Christmas miracle.

"She went to the laundry room," Cooper explained. "But me and Tyler found this cool website that shows you how you can make any gingerbread house you want if you upload a picture, so we can take one of our house and make—"

"Cooper, you need to shut up for five seconds," Lila snapped. Like she wanted to hear anything about Cooper and his dorky BFF, Tyler, who happened to be Beau's little brother. Cooper and Tyler had gone to preschool together—the same preschool Beau and Lila had attended, way back when. Back when she was too young to really know how to make friends.

"But we could make it as a surprise for Mom and Dad—"

"God!" Lila groaned, cutting him off again. "We'll bake cookies or something, but *not* if you're going to be this annoying, okay? It's my vacation, too. Go away."

Cooper just stood there and stared at her, looking like he'd been kicked. With a steel-toed boot. Finally, he scampered off, his shoulders slumped in disappointment.

Lila heaved a sigh. She didn't have time to worry about his little eight-year-old feelings—she had a party to plan. Her delivery of booze was supposed to come in an hour. She checked the delicate gold watch Erik had given her when he left for college. *So you'll always know how long until we see each other again,* he'd said. She felt herself calm down at the thought of his broad, confident smile.

Twelve thirty-two.

T-minus twenty-eight minutes to her parents' departure time.

And then the games would begin. *Finally.*

3

"And Cooper is *not* to bike over to Tyler's house alone. I'm leaving my car, and you'll give him rides if he wants to go over there. Is that clear?" Mrs. Beckwith paused in the act of wrapping a gray scarf around her neck to frown directly at Lila, as if the point needed extra emphasis. Lila shifted her weight from one bare foot to the other, flexing her arches against the glossy hardwood floor of the front hall.

"It's clear, Mom," Lila said, her eyes actually hurting from the effort of *not* rolling them to the back of her head. "I'll give Cooper rides." She was actually more than happy to give Cooper a ride to Tyler's—at least tonight, to get him out of the house. Sleepover for him, party for her.

Her cell phone was vibrating like crazy in her pocket, with everyone no doubt wanting to confirm plans. Yet, her parents were hanging around like they didn't have somewhere else to be. *Come on, come on, come on,* she chanted silently, urging them out the door.

"That goes for you too, Lila," her father chimed in, frowning as he adjusted his Detroit Tigers baseball cap on his balding head. He'd grown up in the Midwest and still proudly supported his hometown sports teams. "Don't think this means you can have Erik up to your room. You know the rules."

Her parents actually loved Erik, despite all the rules. They'd treated Beau like a ticking teenage time bomb. If they were still together, her room would probably be equipped with a nanny cam.

"Erik isn't home from college yet," Lila assured her father, trying to sound trustworthy. She focused on the T-shirt he wore beneath his button-down, featuring a giant pi sign. God, her father was a dork. "So no need to worry about any of that."

"Don't let Cooper stay up all night or gorge himself," Mrs. Beckwith continued. "You can have pizza *or* sugared cereal tomorrow, but not both. And *do not* let him watch scary movies! He'll have nightmares for weeks."

"You guys, I live here," Lila pointed out. Her stomach tightened at the identical frozen glare her parents both aimed at her. She shrugged. "I mean, I know how to take care of Cooper. I'm going to be eighteen in, like, five minutes."

"You are not eighteen yet," her father said. A smile played at the corners of his mouth, like he found her funny. "Adulthood doesn't just happen because you want it to. And I'd mind your attitude if you ever want to see that car."

Lila wanted that car. She could *taste* that car. She didn't care what it looked like or what kind it was—she only cared that it had four wheels, an engine, and locks to keep the rest of them out.

And, okay, if it happened to be a shiny, black, convertible VW Beetle, that wouldn't suck, either.

So, just like every other time they'd dangled this particular carrot in front of her, she pictured her pretty little dream car, and she caved.

"Sorry," Lila said carefully, swallowing her seething resentment. "I just—he's going to be fine. We're going to be safe. Everything's under control. Okay?"

Her parents exchanged a look, and Lila worried she'd blown it. But then her mother's face softened and she leaned over to kiss Lila's cheek, her floral perfume wafting through the air.

"We'll check in from the road," she said.

And then—miraculously!—her parents turned toward the door. Lila could actually *see* her perfect party materialize before her, like a montage scene in a movie. Carly would sweep inside the arched entryway with her favorite cupcakes from Sprinkles in Beverly Hills because, as she always said, nothing cried *party* more than a perfect cupcake. Yoon and

Rebecca would come next, arm in arm and giggling, determined to flirt outrageously with as many cute boys as possible in their ongoing battle for boy-domination. Jeannine would park herself near the door and offer a running commentary on everyone who entered, like North Valley High's very own Joan Rivers (minus the old age and multiple plastic surgeries). It was happening at last!

And then Cooper ran into the front hall, heading straight to their mom. Lila thought he was going for an extra hug or a last whine. But instead of wrapping himself around their mother's waist like a barnacle, Cooper stretched up on his tiptoes and whispered into her ear.

Lila felt a sinking sensation in her belly as her mother's face paled, and her cold blue eyes shot accusingly to Lila's.

"A *party*?" she demanded, horrified. "In this house? Lila, tell me this isn't true!"

Lila's heart plummeted through her body and slammed into her feet with a sickening thud. All feeling deserted her fingers and toes as her pulse pounded out her horror. The last time she'd felt this nauseated was in the seventh grade, when Beau had goaded her into riding that horrible Riddler coaster at Six Flags Magic Mountain.

"What?" Lila asked weakly, but she'd never been much of a spontaneous liar. Give her some time and a good story and she could work an angle. But right now she was like Bambi, eye to eye with a speeding Hummer. "I don't know what Cooper's talking about," she managed to say. *Lame.*

"She was IMing her friends," Cooper piped up, his little voice sounding angelic. He even looked like a cherub, his cheeks rosy and his dark eyes sparkling. Lila wanted to murder him. Could angels be killed? "She said you were leaving and she wanted the party to start as soon as possible."

Lila felt her mouth drop open, but no sound came out. Her mother's lips were pursed. Her father's face turned purplish-red with fury. Their tempers had officially entered the red zone.

"Lila!" Mr. Beckwith boomed. He jabbed a finger at his daughter. "You can forget about that car! You'll be lucky if I give you a ride in *my* car!"

"How could you think you could get away with this?" her mother cried, also at top volume. She threw her hands in the air. "How will we ever trust you again?"

"I was just IMing Carly," Lila protested, thinking quickly. "We were talking about *maybe* watching a movie together, that's all. Not a real party!"

But the word *party* was a bomb, dropped into the middle of her life. The damage was already done.

"How can we go to Phoenix now?" Mr. Beckwith said. "We expect more from you than this, Lila."

Well, that part was true. They *expected* her to be absolutely

100 percent perfect at all times, at school and at home and every-where else. They *expected* her never to ask for help or make a mistake or even act like she might need a hug. She could write a whole book on their expectations.

"Aunt Lucy is expecting us," Mrs. Beckwith replied, angrily. "She's had her thirtieth anniversary party planned for a year." She slashed a hand through the air as if she couldn't hold her temper inside. "This is *outrageous*, Lila! We *trusted* you!"

Cooper just stood there with that smirk on his supposedly so innocent little face, without a care in the world, *reveling* in the scene unfolding in front of him. Lila wanted to smack that smirk into next week, sending Cooper right along with it—

"So, Cooper is obviously perfect and completely trustworthy no matter what, and no one trusts me at all. He could say I was a serial killer and you'd believe him." Lila sniffed, trying to cover her panic with bluster. "Good to know."

"Don't you dare blame your brother!" Lila's mother cried. "If I hear of any retaliation, Lila, you will find yourself grounded for the rest of your senior year. I mean it. Behave *perfectly* for the rest of this weekend and I'll *consider* un-grounding you before spring break."

That took a moment to sink in, and Lila crossed her arms over her chest to keep from hitting something. Or *someone*. Someone significantly shorter than her.

"Meaning I'm already grounded," she translated, her voice

tight and strangled. "Because Cooper invaded my privacy and misinterpreted something he wasn't even supposed to read."

"We *will* be calling," Mrs. Beckwith said, overenunciating each word. She gave Lila the steely stare she'd perfected at her law office, where her underlings raced to do her bidding. "I expect you to pick up when we do. That cell phone had better not be turned off. Are we clear?"

Yes, they were clear. Clearly overreacting. You'd think she'd tried to drown Cooper in the La Brea Tar Pits.

But Lila knew she couldn't say any of that. She'd lost, and it was time to suck it up.

"You are clear," she replied, uncrossing her arms. "I didn't do anything, so please, call all you want."

Cooper received hugs and kisses, Lila received glares and threats, and then the door thudded shut behind them.

Finally, they were gone. But the party was dead.

And so was Lila's social life.

She turned very slowly and let her gaze fall on her little brother.

"You can't take it out on me!" Cooper cried immediately, his brown eyes wide. "Mom said!"

"What's the matter with you?" she asked him, her voice practically a whisper. Her hands curled into fists at her sides.

"I'll tell if you do anything to me!" he yelled. "And then you know they'll *never* give you a car!"

Lila's anger was like a burning flame in her gut. She could feel it searing through her, eating her alive. She didn't care that her brother had once been a preemie, or that their parents thought he needed special treatment for the rest of his life to make up for it. She wanted, *needed*, to retaliate. But she knew he was right—do anything to their beloved Cooper, and she'd be taking the bus to Stanford in the fall.

But suddenly, she had an idea.

Without another word, she turned on her heel and stalked through the house. The light slap of bare feet on the blond wood floor told her Cooper was following.

"What are you doing?" he asked nervously. Good. He *should* be nervous. Other older siblings, those not under direct threat from their parents, would be kicking his puny little ass right about now.

Lila rooted around in her school bag and pulled out her earth science homework. *Thank you, Mr. Geary, for this boring article.* She glanced over the text, confirming that it said exactly what she thought it did: The North Pole was melting thanks to global warming. It even had a satisfyingly dramatic title, perfect for her current purposes: *Who Will Save Santa?*

She reached over and dropped the article in front of Cooper on the coffee table. It landed soundlessly on the glass. She couldn't even be accused of *handing* the article to him. She had simply been doing her homework, she would say, and how could she possibly control Cooper from reading things he shouldn't?

Cooper's eyes fell to the article on the table in front of him. He looked at Lila warily.

She folded her arms, silently daring him.

Cooper snatched up the article, and started to read. Seconds later, his cherubic face fell, and a look of horror settled over his features.

True horror.

Good.

Lila felt triumph soar through her.

Merry Christmas, you little brat, she thought smugly, and stormed out of the room.

4

BECKWITH HOUSE
LOS ANGELES
DECEMBER 22
3:23 P.M.

Damage control consisted of a few e-mails and a whole lot of unpleasant conversations as Lila called her party off—none more unpleasant than her parents' multiple check-in calls. At least she had some privacy for a change. Cooper had asked to go over to Tyler's house after the global-warming bomb she'd dropped on him. She hadn't even minded driving him over there in her mother's car—at this rate, Lila would be geriatric before she had a car of her own—because he'd looked so obviously dejected. It was exactly what he deserved for being a tattling little brat.

"It sucks," Lila said into the phone now. She was sprawled across the daybed at the top of the stairs, peering out the window. Below, the grassy lawn stretched from the bright purple bougainvillea vines that crawled along the side of the house to the street shaded with big oak trees out front. It was her favorite spot in the house.

"This is just so *lame*," Yoon moaned. Again. "Why are your parents so freaking uptight?"

"I wish I knew," Lila said sourly, though she wasn't 100 percent sure she liked Yoon criticizing her family. It was one thing when Carly did it—she and Lila were practically family themselves. But Yoon didn't get a free pass just because they were in the same clique.

On the other hand, Lila couldn't deny the fact that her parents *were* pretty freaking uptight.

She tilted her head back and scowled at the popcorn ceiling, switching the bulky white house phone from one shoulder to the other. Her cell phone got zero reception in this part of the house, and she'd decided she deserved some comfort while mopping up the sad remains of her abruptly canceled party. Yoon sighed heavily. "I refuse to accept that your annoying little brother can just ruin all your plans in three seconds!"

"It's like the purpose of his entire existence," Lila deadpanned. But she felt a little prickle of unease move through her, a sudden urge to defend Cooper to Yoon. She slapped it away like some annoying insect. Cooper deserved whatever he got.

"Huh." Yoon blew out a breath. "You know, maybe this doesn't have to be a *total* disaster."

"What, do you have a time machine?" Lila laughed at the

idea. Would she go beam back to right before Cooper decided to tattle? Or to right before she told him to leave her alone, provoking him to retaliate? Or maybe she would go back to this afternoon, when she'd still thought Erik would be in town by now and she'd *known* that her party was going to kick ass. It felt like a million years ago already.

Or maybe she could go all the way back to before Cooper was born. When her parents didn't lavish all of their love and attention on him, leaving Lila with only lectures and threats.

"Well, not exactly a *time machine*," Yoon said, the faintest note of calculation in her voice. "But how about a change of venue?"

"What do you mean?" Lila asked, an uneasy feeling spreading through her. She had a feeling she knew the answer to that question.

"I mean, would you mind if *I* threw a party tonight, instead?" Yoon asked sweetly. So sweetly that Lila immediately wondered if that was why Yoon hadn't answered when Lila first called. She'd probably cooked this up with her usual partner in crime, Rebecca, before calling Lila back.

"Well—" Lila began.

"Rebecca and I were so bummed that the biggest party of the year was just *canceled*, you know?" Yoon continued hurriedly, confirming her suspicions. "And then it occurred to us that *my* parents are out of town like always, and why should all your awesome planning go to waste just because your little brother can't keep his mouth shut? It can still totally be your party, Lila, but just at my house instead of yours." She paused. "I mean, if you're okay with it. I'll understand if you want to bail on the whole thing at this point."

Lila sighed. It wasn't like she could force Yoon not to have a party—especially when she was confined to house arrest until her parents returned on Sunday.

"Go ahead," she said into the phone, glad her friend couldn't see the face she was making right now. She looked at her reflection in the window, wrinkling up her forehead and sticking out her tongue like a gargoyle. "Someone should profit from my awesome party-planning skills." She let out a little laugh.

Yoon's return trill of laughter was equally fake. "Awesome!" she squealed. "And don't worry if you can't come—I'll post all the pictures on Facebook!"

Lila hung up the phone and lay there for a moment, stretched out on the daybed, feeling sorry for herself. She glanced at the watch that wasn't bringing Erik closer after all, and heaved a sigh. It was almost three thirty—time to pick Cooper up. Her reprieve was over.

But she couldn't bring herself to move just yet. Right now she was *supposed* to be slipping into her cute little Betsey Johnson dress, royal blue, tight in all the right places. She was supposed to be meeting Erik at the door, where he'd cover her with kisses.

She was supposed to be greeting her friends and classmates, being toasted and complimented, being lauded as the pretty, perfect, popular girl she'd worked so hard to be.

Instead, *Yoon* was throwing the party of the year, while Lila was forced to spend the weekend with her baby brother, fielding angry phone calls from her parents every five minutes.

Merry Christmas to me.

Cooper, naturally, did not come running outside when Lila honked the horn, as she had specifically ordered him to do when she'd dropped him off.

Of course not. Why should he do anything to make Lila's life easier?

Lila muttered angrily to herself as she parked her mother's car in the street and climbed out into the chilly afternoon air. The sun was already starting to head for the horizon, even though it was barely three thirty, and it was cold. Well, California cold. Lila's father had grown up in Michigan, and he liked to talk about *real cold* whenever someone complained about the mild L.A. winters.

Lila was a native Californian, meaning anything below seventy degrees was shiver-worthy. She tightened her bright pink scarf around her neck as she walked up Beau's driveway. Even the hot anger at Cooper pulsing through her veins didn't warm her up.

She reached the Hodgeses' front door and took a deep breath before knocking. No one answered. She knocked again, with more force.

"Why am I not surprised?" she asked the late-afternoon sun. It wasn't shocking that the doorbell's chime was being neglected. The truth was that the Hodges family had kind of been in disarray ever since Mr. and Mrs. Hodges had divorced a few years back. Lila could remember how withdrawn and moody Beau had become as things got worse between his parents. And how he'd become even colder and weirder after the divorce.

Lila reached out and tried the door. It fell open. For a moment, she wondered if Cooper and Tyler might be setting her up with some elaborate revenge scenario. Cooper might be a naive little brat who still believed in Santa Claus, but he was also pretty clever. Just last summer he'd rigged up a pulley system outside her bedroom door that had hurled a mesh bag filled with little rubber insects at her face when she'd staggered out one Sunday morning.

Lila eased inside the house and closed the door behind her. No rubber bugs. No sign of anything or anybody else, either. She cocked her head to the side to listen. She expected to hear the usual sounds of Cooper and Tyler playing—high-pitched whoops and cries as they played Wii in the den or small explosions as they concocted bizarre potions in Tyler's science lab of a bedroom. But all was silent.

"Cooper?" She called out, and then waited. "Cooper!"

Silence.

Lila stood for a moment at the base of the stairs, but she couldn't hear anything from the rooms above, and she knew it was highly unlikely that two eight-year-old boys were quietly reading. They were like wild animals, always moving around and getting into things, like, for instance, Lila's closet. The den was empty of everything save for the flashing screen saver on the family computer. It was a picture of Beau and Tyler, happy and carefree on a beach somewhere. She averted her eyes from Beau's shirtless, surprisingly buff form, like it was something she wasn't supposed to see.

Lila had just wandered into the kitchen when she heard the sounds of muffled music. It seemed to waft up from the floorboards below her feet.

She crossed the kitchen in a few quick steps and wrenched open the door to the basement. She catapulted down the rickety steps, the sound of electric guitar humming directly into her nerves. Into her *last* nerve, to be precise. She made it to the bottom of the steps and turned the corner.

Beau was standing with his back to her in the sparsely furnished basement, headphones clamped to his ears, the electric guitar wailing. Everything about him made her stomach twist with rage and regret. Rage that he dressed like a homeless person, deliberately. Regret that when she'd been with him, she had too, and she hadn't known any better. She hated his black jeans. His torn T-shirt. The smooth muscles of his biceps that he by no means deserved. A hot body was wasted on Beau Hodges, since he chose to dress like someone who ought to be pasty and soft and gross. He cradled that guitar of his like it was a newborn.

"Turn that down!" she yelled repeatedly. Finally he turned and saw her standing there. His blue eyes looked resigned and mocking. They always did when he looked at her.

"What do you want, Lila?" he asked as he pulled the headphones off and let them hang around his neck. His voice was gruff, and he made no attempt to hide the fact that her presence was about as welcome as a swarm of hornets. He put his guitar down in its stand and then ran his hands through his shaggy, black hair. Lila's own hands itched with the need to cut his raggedy mane. He looked like a recalcitrant sheep.

"What do you think I want?" Lila snapped at him. She jabbed a finger up toward the rest of the house. "I can't find my brother."

"What do you mean, you can't find him?" Beau sounded half amused and half bored. "Are they playing hide-and-seek? Tyler always hides in the attic."

"I mean," she said, overenunciating each word, "that he isn't here. And neither is Tyler, for that matter."

"They were playing video games fifteen minutes ago," Beau said with a *not my problem* shrug. The classic Beau Hodges response to anything and everything.

"Well, they aren't playing video games now," Lila replied. She eyed his surroundings: a makeshift practice room complete with a bass, a keyboard, and a few amps strewn about. A vintage poster of the Dead Kennedys was taped to the basement wall. She focused her attention back on Beau and crossed her arms. "Are you sure it was only fifteen minutes since you saw them? You don't really keep track of time when you're *playing guitar*, do you?" Her voice oozed with sarcasm, to drive home how little she thought of his *playing guitar.*

Beau looked at her like he wanted to kill her. With his hands. His eyes narrowed and his mouth flattened. "Fine," he said, in a remarkably calm tone. "Let's go find them."

He brushed past her and headed up the rickety basement stairs, taking them two at a time.

They searched every room in the house, including the attic, calling out each boy's name and looking everywhere—under beds and in closets and even in Beau's bedroom, where Lila hadn't been in years and was sure she didn't want to be now. It looked exactly the same. It even smelled the same—like Dial soap and sweat, which should have been grosser than it really was. Lila could swear she saw a ghost of her old self in the corner, dancing like the freak she'd been to one of Beau's silly tunes. She shook it off. There was nothing of her here. Not anymore.

"They're gone," Beau finally muttered, after they searched the pantry and in the crawl space behind the washing machine in the laundry room.

Lila closed her eyes. It was as if all the events of the day were whirling around in a ball inside of her, tangled and jagged, and now Cooper was *missing*, and she wanted to hurl the whole messy thing at Beau's head. "This is all your fault!" she cried.

"My fault?" His blue eyes met hers. "How exactly is this my fault? Please, do tell," he asked quizzically.

"You left them all alone! They're *eight years old* and now they're *gone!*"

Lila words sounded familiar as they ricocheted around Beau's front hallway. They were exactly what she imagined her mother would say if she was standing there—except her mother would direct the words at Lila, not Beau. So now she was channeling her mother, too. Fantastic.

"You need to calm down." There was an angry light in his eyes, and she could see that he was fighting to maintain his cool.

"Oh, sure," she bit out, amped up for a fight. She could use one right about now. "I'll just chill out while my little brother is *God knows where* when I'm supposed to be taking care of him for the weekend. I'll be sure to explain that you suggested that to my parents—"

"Stop." Beau held up a hand. "I'm sure it makes you feel better to yell at me, but it's not helping anything. My mom's out of town too, so I'm in the same boat, here. We need to think clearly, not freak out."

Lila blinked, taken aback. "Since when did you become Mr. Maturity?" she asked. The Beau she knew was an obnoxious holier-than-thou jerk who could argue until he was blue in the face, just because he couldn't bear to be wrong about anything. *That* Beau had never once, in all the time she'd known him, backed down from even the slightest, most inconsequential challenge.

"Since I had no other freaking choice," he muttered, and then turned and headed toward the den. Confused, Lila trailed after him.

She stood in the doorway as Beau glanced around the room, like he was trying to piece together their brothers' last moments in the house. He crossed the den in a few quick strides and stood over the computer desk. He tapped the space bar, and the hulking desktop computer came to life. On the screen, Google Maps loomed large.

Lila drifted over, and stared over Beau's shoulder. A Google Maps journey was plotted out, with the blue line stretching all the way from Los Angeles up the edge of the United States, into Canada, and then even higher.

"What the hell?" Beau sounded baffled.

Lila's eyes flicked to the end of the long blue line.

Destination: the North Pole.

She stared. The earth science article she'd handed Cooper flashed before her eyes. *Who Will Save Santa?*

Oh, crap.

5

"Oh my God," Lila said in amazement, shaking her head as if the motion would help the ridiculousness of this situation sink in. "Cooper and Tyler are going to save Santa!"

"They're *what*?" Beau asked, shifting away from her. They'd been standing close together to look at the computer, their hips nearly touching. Lining the desk were framed snapshots of Beau and Tyler over the last couple of years. One, from when they were younger, had clearly been cropped to cut their dad out of the picture.

Lila took a step back from Shaggy Doo, and told him all about Cooper ratting her out and her subtle retaliation.

When she was finished, Beau just stood there, looking at her.

"What?" she demanded, bristling.

"Really?" He shook his head. "You decided that the appropriate response to an eight-year-old tattling on you was to threaten to kill Santa Claus?"

"It's not my fault he's a moron. Did you believe in Santa Claus when you were eight?" Lila scoffed.

"I didn't, no," Beau said quietly. Something about the look in his eyes made a spiral of shame curl through her gut. "But I wanted to. Didn't you?"

"Spare me the lecture, please," Lila snapped, shoving away the sudden pang of guilt. "I don't expect you to understand. I'm sure you think all parties should be canceled because you hate people. And fun."

"This isn't about your party," Beau retorted, his voice taking on that familiar critical edge that Lila remembered. "Although I'm sure having the entire lacrosse team puke their guts out in your mother's rosebushes would be like nirvana for you." He rolled his eyes. "This is about the fact that you think it's okay to treat your brother like that. He's just a kid."

"He's a pain in the ass," Lila said dismissively. She raised her eyebrows at him, in challenge. "And right now he's missing, so—"

"Yeah, as a direct result of what you did," Beau interrupted with a short laugh. "Nice job, Lila. Maybe next time he does something you don't like you can cut all the crap and just tell him you took Santa out yourself with an AK-47. Or maybe you can just kick a few puppies. Better yet: Tell him what really happens to stray dogs at the pound."

"How is this my fault when *you're* the one who lost them?" Lila asked, her voice razor sharp. She reached into the pocket of her faded Lucky jeans for her cell phone. "As delightful as it is debating with you, I think maybe we should just find our brothers, don't you?"

But her cell phone wasn't in her pocket. She frowned, trying to remember the last time she'd seen it. She hadn't used it earlier—she'd made calls on the house phone. In fact, the last time she remembered seeing her cell, she'd been dropping Cooper off. The phone had buzzed to indicate she'd had a text, and she'd ignored it, because she just wanted to get Cooper out of her face for a while.

She knew it wasn't in the car. She could visualize the little black plastic bucket between the front seats, and it was empty.

A new thought hit her then.

"I think Cooper took my phone," she said, letting her empty hands drop against her thighs. She groaned. "*God!* What is the *matter* with him?"

"For one thing, he thinks he has to save Santa Claus," Beau said dryly.

"I have an idea," Lila snapped. "How about you do something useful and call my cell phone to see if he answers?"

"I'm not the one who traumatized the poor kid, and my

brother, too, no doubt, with a scary article on global warming," Beau said, but he pulled out his iPhone. It wasn't until he punched in her name and made the call that it occurred to her to wonder why he still had her number saved.

On the very rare occasions Lila had to call Beau to schedule some Cooper-related activity, she had to look the number up in her mother's paper address book. She'd removed Beau's name and number from her own cell years ago. Deliberately. Like she needed Mr. Doom and Gloom on speed dial when she had a new life filled with fun, happy people who threw parties and enjoyed themselves.

"It's ringing," Beau said. He eyed her. "Thank God you don't have one of those phones that plays a song selection instead of a ring. I don't think I could handle Jessica Simpson right now."

"Ha-ha," Lila deadpanned, suddenly glad that Cooper had her phone, so Beau couldn't hear that her ringtone was the latest Justin Timberlake song. Not that she cared what he thought, but she couldn't handle a lecture about what constituted good music according to Beau right now.

"No answer," Beau said, punching the off button. He crossed his arms over his chest and cocked an eyebrow at her. "What now?"

She loved how he did that—threw the ball squarely in her court. Like it was up to her to figure it out because *he* couldn't watch two kids for a couple of hours. Not that this surprised

Lila in the least. She'd always had to initiate everything during their relationship. She'd even instigated their first kiss!

Not that this was the time to be thinking about that.

"Why are you looking at me like that?" Beau asked, puzzled.

"Like what?" It was like when faced with this much exposure to Beau, she reverted to the last time they'd had this much sustained interaction: freshman year. When all she'd wanted to do was scream at him until he changed his depressing downward trajectory.

"Like you want to yell at me."

"I don't want to yell at you," Lila lied. She rubbed at her temples, fighting off an impending Cooper and Beau–related headache. "I don't care about you enough to yell at you. I just want to find my brother and go home and read about the party I'm supposed to be having via other people's Tweets okay?"

But when she looked back at Beau, there was the oddest expression on his face, almost as if she'd hurt his feelings. Then his phone beeped and the usual mocking look returned.

Lila glared at the iPhone.

"Is it him?" she demanded. "He totally stole my phone, didn't he?"

"Uh, yeah," Beau said, his attention on the screen. He shook his head. "And that's pretty much the least of our problems right now."

He held out the phone so Lila could read the text Cooper

had sent: WE'RE GOING TO THE NORTH POLE TO SAVE SANTA—BACK IN TIME FOR XMAS.

"I'm going to kill him!" She snatched the phone out of Beau's hand. She punched the buttons to redial her own cell phone, her anger mounting with each ring.

"Um, hello?" came a voice, high and giggling.

"You're dead, Cooper," Lila snapped at him. "Do you understand me? Tell me where you are!"

"Good idea," Beau said sarcastically, standing right next to her. "Threaten him. That should do the trick."

Lila turned her back on him. "Cooper!" she yelled. "I'm serious!"

But all she heard in reply was laughter.

Beau reached over and plucked the phone from Lila's fingers. "Cooper," he said into the phone. "Put Tyler on." He paused. Then, in a much friendlier tone than the one he'd been using on Lila, he said, "Tyler, man, where are you guys? Mom's going to freak."

Lila couldn't stand the fact that she couldn't hear what Tyler was saying, so she moved closer to Beau, sticking her head next to his so she could hear. He threw a startled look her way, but tilted the phone toward her.

"You took a cab, huh? But you can't take one all the way to Santa's. The North Pole is far away, especially for two little guys," Beau continued, reasonably. "Don't you think?"

"It's okay," Tyler piped up. "We can do it."

"We can take care of ourselves!" Cooper said in the background. "Santa needs us!"

"Santa really does need us," Tyler said very seriously. "Someone has to help him."

Lila could feel the glare that Beau leveled at the side of her head. She raised her chin in defiance, but didn't respond.

"If you tell us where you are," she said in a cajoling voice, "maybe we can help you help him."

"We don't need your help!" Cooper cried, and then there was more laughter. Lila was about to lose it and start screaming when another noise sounded in the background.

It was a PA system, and it was very distinct: ALL ABOARD!

"Gotta go!" Tyler said with a giggle, and the line went dead.

Lila and Beau stared at each other for a frozen moment, each waiting to see if the other had heard.

"They took a cab to—" Beau began.

"The train station," Lila finished, hope and relief exploding in her chest.

"Let's go," Beau said at once.

Lila followed him through the house and out the back door into the garage. She was so focused on finding Cooper and putting an end to this nonsense that she barely noticed Beau's beat-up old Escort, complete with the sorts of bumper stickers you'd expect from an angry hipster dude intent on alienating himself from the rest of the world.

She slid into the passenger seat and eyed Beau, who was, after all, the exact sort of scruffy guy you'd expect to be driving this car. She wondered which obscure band he'd tattooed on his back or around his calf in the last few years, and was only mildly surprised that he wasn't sporting more piercings. He still had only the one—a silver hoop in his left ear, attached in the middle instead of the lobe.

She leaned back into the bucket seat and closed her eyes. She just needed to get her hands on Cooper, and then she'd be done with all of this—crappy car, pissy ex-boyfriend, and everything else so typically and annoyingly Beau.

Soon, she thought, *just like our relationship, it will be like none of this ever happened.*

6

"The thing is," Beau said, breaking the tense silence between them as he slammed the car into gear, then gunned it down the driveway and out into the street, "I don't understand what you *thought* was going to happen."

Lila flicked a look at him but didn't answer. His tone did not bode well. It reminded her of many past conversations in which Beau dissected her seemingly endless character flaws. *Yay.* She belted herself into the passenger seat and tried to get warm by rubbing her hands together. The temperature was falling, and the wind was kicking up outside, making the trees sway and rustle. The houses on Beau's street were decked out in Christmas lights, with fake snowmen on the green lawns and reindeer posed beneath the palm trees. It was the start of the holiday weekend, and everyone was preparing to enjoy themselves.

Everyone except Lila.

"I mean, did you even think for five seconds what Cooper might do?" Beau continued. "When you basically told him Santa Claus was in mortal danger?"

Oh, right. She should have guessed immediately. The Beau Hodges Blame Game.

"I don't know," she said, pretending to think it over. Beau drove way too fast down the residential backstreets of their town, headed for the train station at a speed that would get them a hefty speeding ticket if clocked. "I guess I thought that maybe it would be cool to ignore two eight-year-olds for two hours and then act all shocked and surprised that something happened to them while they were unsupervised." She looked at him. "Oh no, wait. That's you."

"I'm not the one who provoked them!" Beau barely halted at a stop sign and then floored the gas pedal through an intersection. Lila's head rocked back against the headrest like they were on a roller coaster. Why was she not surprised that he was a crazy driver?

"Maybe not," Lila said, "but you did ignore them, didn't you?"

Beau turned his right signal on and gunned it around a corner. "Cooper and Tyler have played together, without incident, at least ten million times while I played a little guitar downstairs. Why was today any different? Because Cooper got hit with Hurricane Lila."

"Hurricane Lila," she echoed derisively. "Cute. You have names for me, still. After all these years."

"You didn't think before you dropped the global warming thing on Cooper," Beau said. He was vibrating with tension all of a foot away from her, clearly fighting for control. "You just wanted to hurt him."

"You're right," Lila snapped. "I did. Better he learns now that if you mess with people, you might get messed with in return." She sniffed. "It's practically a public service."

"What about the part where you're *ten years older* than him, and should maybe figure out how to be the bigger person?"

She suddenly remembered their shared art class in sixth grade, when they had to make papier-mâché animals for a class project. Lila's pig had been lopsided and soggy, and in no way resembled a pig of any kind. She thought it was hilarious, and named the lumpy thing Gerald. Beau, on the other hand, had painstakingly constructed a life-size, anatomically correct rooster. Even then, he thought he was better than her.

"Ever considered the possibility that watching the kids might mean, you know, *watching them*?" Lila asked with acid sweetness. "Instead of hiding in your basement pretending someone cares if you can play all of 'Jesus of Suburbia'?"

"You know what, Lila?" Beau's voice was angry and tight. Lila knew she'd scored a direct hit, and wished that felt a little more satisfying. "I think maybe we should both just shut up."

Lila pursed her lips but didn't say another word as Beau careened into the train station parking lot. They leaped out of the car as soon as it screeched to a stop, and sprinted toward the station doors. Beau ran ahead of her, his lanky legs taking long strides. He wasn't even a little breathless when they got inside. Their eyes wildly searched the nearly empty terminal. The long rows of plastic seats were dotted with only a few commuters, most reading the newspaper or quietly talking on the phone.

Lila scanned and re-scanned the scene, seeing only the same handful of people, none of them two mischievous little boys. "I don't see them," she said angrily. "What are we going to do?"

"I don't know," he replied in a similar, clipped tone. He jerked his chin in the direction of a nearby Amtrak worker. "Maybe somebody noticed them."

Lila followed him over to a woman in an Amtrak uniform, with the biggest, roundest, red hair she had ever seen. It sky-rocketed off her head and was hair-sprayed into a glossy bouf-fant. Lila had to force herself not to stare openly.

"I'm sorry to bother you," Beau said, with an easy politeness. Lila gaped. Since when was Beau charming? "But have you seen two little boys running around here, by any chance? All alone?"

"They're both about this big," Lila chimed in, holding her hand just above her waist. "One wears Harry Potter glasses, and the other one has a mess of freckles and was wearing a bright green sweatshirt."

"I was wondering who was supposed to be with those two," the older woman replied, shaking her head. Her gaze turned faintly accusing. "They had online tickets, but they seemed a little young to be traveling to Seattle all by themselves."

"Seattle?" Lila could not possibly have heard that right. She ignored the accusing look and matching tone from Mrs. Red Round Hair, and focused on the part that did not make any sense at all. The part that *could not* make any sense. "Did you say they were going to *Seattle*?"

Beau closed his eyes for a moment. He ran his hands through his hair, which Lila remembered he did when he was agitated. Like when his dog had run away back in the sixth grade and he'd maintained a tense nightly vigil for two weeks until Fender had come back. Or when she'd demanded he explain *why* he refused to go to Carly's birthday party in the ninth grade, and *I hate zombies* didn't count. He'd looked her straight in the eyes and said, *Because I'll hate you, too.*

"They got on the Coast Starlight service headed north," the woman said, looking back and forth between Lila and Beau. "Final destination is Seattle. It runs daily."

"Seattle," Lila said again, as if saying it out loud might change the end result somehow. "As in, Washington state. That Seattle."

"Thank you," Beau said to the Amtrak worker, giving her another polite smile. He turned to Lila when the woman walked away and raised an eyebrow. "'*That* Seattle'? Is there another Seattle that I don't know about?"

"There's no time for mockery!" Lila snapped at him, her mind racing. If Cooper was going to *Seattle*, how could she possibly keep that from her parents? He was on a *train*! Anything could happen!

She ran over to the big display of train schedules near the information booth. She scanned the colorful pamphlets and snagged one that read *Coast Starlight* across the top. She glanced at it quickly, then took off toward the train station's tall front doors, headed for the parking lot.

Beau followed.

"What exactly are we doing?" he asked, still not breathing heavily.

"Simi Valley is the next station," Lila replied, puffing a little bit. And she actually ran a few miles every other day. She didn't know why it was suddenly so important to her that she be more athletic than Beau. "If we hurry, maybe we can catch them there."

She made it to the passenger side of his ratty old car and waited impatiently for him to unlock it. He had to climb inside and reach across the seat to do so by hand.

"I'm not sure chasing a train across the Valley is the best idea here," Beau said, resting his palms against the steering wheel. What he was notably *not* doing was driving his car.

"Beau!" Lila stomped the floor of the car, wishing she could

move it forward herself, like the Flintstones' Stone Age car—
which was probably better-made than this wreck of a vehicle.
"Come *on!*"

Beau started the Escort and backed out of his parking spot,
but he was frowning.

"I think maybe we should face the fact that this is out of control," he said as he started to drive through the side streets that
surrounded the train station. It was still the afternoon, and the
real L.A. traffic thankfully hadn't kicked in. Yet. "We're talking
about two eight-year-olds. This isn't, like, a Disney movie or
something where a talking dog will lead them to safety."

"And you are definitely no Zac Efron," Lila said, smirking
as she tried to imagine Beau in *High School Musical*. Or even
watching *High School Musical*.

He ignored her. "I think maybe we should call the police,
Lila. Do they put out Amber Alerts for missing kids even if you
know it's not an abduction or whatever?"

Oh my God, police? Lila thought she might have a heart
attack. The police would want to talk to the boys' guardians,
wouldn't they? That meant hunting down her parents at Aunt
Lucy's house in Phoenix, and *that* meant total and utter disaster. Look what had happened when they'd found out about
the party! Lila couldn't imagine what they would do if they
discovered Cooper had embarked on *interstate*—and possibly
international— travel.

"We can't call the police," she said in a flat, no-arguments tone. She and Beau would simply have to find the boys themselves.

"We can't?" Beau threw a look at her. "Um, why is that?"

"All you need to do here is drive fast, okay?" Lila rubbed at her arms. "We'll head them off at the next station. We'll get them back safe and sound, with absolutely no reason whatsoever to call the police. Except maybe for when I kill Cooper with my bare hands."

Beau looked skeptical. "Isn't that what you're supposed to do when kids go missing?" he asked. "Call the cops?"

"They're not missing!" Lila yelped. "We know exactly where they are!" *Still* he frowned in that way that signaled he didn't agree with her. "Listen, Beau," she said urgently. "What's the first thing the police are going to do? After they intercept the boys wherever?" She made an impatient noise when he didn't respond. "They'll tell our parents." She shuddered, and not for effect. "It will be carnage. The total and utter end of me."

"I thought you said they're already pissed at you," Beau pointed out with a shrug, like the end of Lila was not something that overly concerned him. "Isn't that why you stomped all over Cooper's Santa fantasy in the first place?"

"Getting tattled on for allegedly, *maybe* throwing a party is one thing," Lila said darkly. "Getting called by the police because

Cooper took off on a train to Seattle? They'll ground me for the next eighteen years. I'll never go to Stanford, and I will never, ever be the proud owner of a convertible VW Beetle."

"A car?" Beau frowned deeper, his mouth curling derisively. "You're worried about getting a *car*?"

"Easy for you to say, since you have one," Lila retorted. She wrinkled up her nose as she looked around at his version of a vehicle. *Sort of.*

She blew out a frustrated sigh. "Listen, Beau, your mom has always been way more chill than mine. Remember when we snuck out to see that movie in eighth grade? I was grounded for two weeks and had to do *yard work*. Your mom just laughed." At the time, she'd thought that the punishment was worth getting to be out so late with Beau. Now she couldn't imagine pulling a single weed just to spend a few minutes with him. "But do you really want her to know that you lost Tyler and he's now on a *train*? To another state?"

"No," he said quietly after a moment, surprising her straight down to the soles of her boots. "I don't."

Something about the way he said it made her wonder if something else was going on. But maybe she was just imagining it. She shifted around so she could look at him as the streets zipped by outside the window, one ranch-style split-level after another. The only thing that really distinguished the houses were their varying front-yard holiday decorations. "I mean, it would be different if they were really missing," she said. "But we know they're on that train. They're, like, contained."

This time when Beau looked over at her, his eyes were crinkled up a bit in the corners, like he wanted to smile but wasn't letting himself.

"You can stop the hard sell," he said gently. "I'm not arguing about it. I'm driving."

"Okay, then," Lila said, feeling suddenly off-center. She looked away, at the red taillights of the car ahead of them as they raced west. "So—drive faster!" she ordered him, hunching down in her seat. "We have a train to catch."

7

ROAD TO SIMI VALLEY
LOS ANGELES
DECEMBER 22
4:01 P.M.

Three minutes later, Lila thought she might have to reach over and strangle Beau and then throw his body out of the window toward the foothills of the Santa Susana Mountains that loomed in the north. Or even the Simi Hills to the south—she wasn't picky.

"What are you doing?" she asked when he zoomed past yet another entrance to the freeway. What was the matter with him? Didn't he know where he was going? Everybody knew the quickest way to Simi Valley from their hometown in the San Fernando Valley was the 118 Freeway that curved through the mountains separating them.

Everybody but Beau, apparently.

"Um, I'm driving." Beau didn't spare Lila a glance. He just slouched there, one wrist falling over the top of the steering wheel and the other in his lap. So nonchalant, like he wasn't, in fact, racing a train across California.

"You just missed the freeway," she pointed out, trying to sound calm. "Twice."

"I didn't 'miss' the freeway." Now he looked at her, his dark eyebrows high, like she was the one acting crazy. She could see a gleam of that mocking blue, and it immediately made her shoulders tense up. "I don't like the freeways."

"You don't *like* them," Lila repeated, as if she couldn't understand the words without sounding them out. "Nobody *likes* the freeway, Beau. But it does happen to be the quickest route between point A and point B."

Beau snorted like that was the most ridiculous thing he'd ever heard in his life. "Sure, if there's no traffic, the freeway is great. But when does that ever happen? It's always a parking lot."

"So we're going to miss this train because you have some philosophical objection to the *possibility* of traffic on the 118?" Lila asked. She shook her head, her knee jogging up and down in place. "That's a great plan. Really."

"It's not a philosophical objection. It's a practical objection," Beau retorted. "Surface streets are faster."

"You live in a fantasy world," Lila replied. "Surface streets have stop signs, traffic lights, not to mention speed limits. Hello."

"I had no idea you were this obsessed with the California

freeway system," Beau said in a dismissive way that burrowed right up under her skin and made her itch—like he was his own personal brand of poison oak and she was particularly allergic. He raked his thick, dark hair back from his face with his free hand.

Lila's jaw clenched and she ground her teeth together. Could Beau be any more condescending?

In a word: yes. He could, as she recalled pretty clearly, set records for being the most condescending, patronizing jerk around. But there was no use in letting the situation go nuclear, as their fights had often gone back in the day. She could remember, in particular, how he'd reacted when he'd found out that she'd gotten together with Erik—the day after breaking up with him.

Congratulations, Lila, he'd drawled, his eyes blazing at her, hotter than the sun above them in the courtyard at lunch. *You're apparently even more vapid and pathetic than you sounded on Friday.*

She'd tried to apologize to him—still feeling badly, at that point, about hurting someone she'd cared about for so long—but he'd brushed her off.

Don't let me hold you back from your glorious destiny as Erik Hollander's latest groupie, he'd said, his voice so sarcastic and cutting that all these years later, the memory of it made her cringe. Lila squeezed her eyes shut for a moment.

She was stuck in this car with him, true, but that was a tem-
porary thing. She hadn't somehow woken up to find herself
back in time, trapped in her going-nowhere relationship with
a guy determined to be as miserable as humanly possible. She
restrained a shudder at the very idea.

The silence dragged out between them as Beau's car raced
through the late afternoon. The hills loomed up on either side
of them in the winding mountain pass, looking almost sinis-
ter against the golden sun in the western sky. Lila checked her
watch: four ten. She tried to pretend that she was somewhere
else, somewhere Beau-less. Like, for example, driving up to her
dorm at Stanford next fall in her shiny new convertible, having left her parents and Cooper and all their assorted expectations behind. She imagined the northern California wind gently
tossing her dark, blown-out hair back and forth. And then she
pictured Erik running toward her across the bright green lawn
of the quad, sweeping her up into his strong arms, twirling her
around, and kissing her long and hard in front of the entire
incoming freshman class.

She heard Beau sigh slightly, and then he clicked on the car
stereo. It was worth significantly more than the car it sat in. He
fiddled with the console, clicking over to his iPod connection.

Good. Lila nodded to herself. *Music will make this all slide
by like a dream—*

But the thought died away as absurd sounds filled the car,

jaunty and bouncy, with a scratchy voice that drowned out everything. It sounded like the circus. Like a creepy, demented circus in a horror movie. Was that an *accordion*?

"What is this?" she demanded. The weird music made her think of old men with thick accents, playing chess in the park in heavy sweaters no matter how hot it was.

"Beirut," Beau said defensively, glaring at the road.

"As in, the music of a foreign culture?"

"As in, that's the name of the band," he shot back. "Which I'm listening to because it's good. Something I realize you don't care about anymore."

"You listen to polka music now?" Lila demanded, scandalized. "Seriously?"

"I forgot to download my Lady Gaga collection," Beau said snidely. "My bad."

"There's nothing wrong with Lady Gaga," Lila snapped at him. "At least she can carry a tune. Unlike *this* crap!" She waved her hand at the stereo. The music now included what sounded like a sitar.

"Fine," Beau said tightly. He punched at the console again, and something more folky—and more melodic, at least—filled the car. "This is Fleet Foxes. They played on *Saturday Night Live* once, so hopefully that won't be too esoteric or weird for you."

"Right," Lila said, not even bothering to roll her eyes. She channeled her annoyance through her voice. "Because if a band you like is even *known* by more than two people, they've sold out and are lame. I forgot."

"I don't like Top Forty music," Beau said, his voice clipped. "So sue me."

"You don't like it because it makes you feel superior not to," Lila countered. "Not because you actually dislike the music. You've probably never listened to a Fergie song in your life."

"Do I really have to listen to every overproduced piece-of-crap song to know they all suck?" Beau asked, and laughed disdainfully. "That they're an offense to anyone who's actually interested in real music?"

"As defined by you, Beau Hodges," Lila pointed out. "You get to decide what's real and what's not. You think it makes you cool to hate on things that other people like."

Lila had no idea why she was acting like pop music was this important to her. It was something in the way Beau dismissed it, like it was *beneath* him—while he was listening to glorified polka music. What gave him the right to decide what was good and what wasn't?

There was another silence between them, as the music soared, surprisingly crisp and beautiful, between them.

"What the hell happened to you?" Beau asked finally, as if the question were being torn from him. Lila had the feeling he would have given a lot not to ask it.

"Britney Spears fried my brain," she replied dryly. "Is that what you want to hear?"

"I'm serious," Beau said, and for once he didn't sound like he was trying to trap her into saying something he could misconstrue. He sounded puzzled. "I mean, you used to love music. You used to live for it. Real music—and now you're mounting a defense of bubblegum pop? I don't get it."

"People change," Lila said. Because there was nothing else to say. How could she explain the choices she'd made? To him, of all people? It either made perfect sense why she'd had to do what she'd done, or it didn't, and no amount of explanation could bridge that gap. It had never made any sense to Beau. Because he was a guy, maybe, but also because he was Beau. And it wasn't about pop music. Obviously. It was about . . . having the kind of life that you could look back on and be proud of. That would make sense on yearbook pages ten years later. She had wanted her life to *matter*.

"Tell me about it," Beau said with another snotty laugh. Because Beau thought even wanting that kind of thing was a sign of weakness. "I guess becoming Miss Popular, Queen of North Valley High, means you have to give up everything you love. Sounds like a great bargain. Really."

"You don't know what you're talking about." She eyed him, taking in the proud, defiant tilt of his chin and the way his dark hair fell so messily over his face and neck, then looked back at the road. The dark pavement stretched out before them, the mountains rising in the distance. The sun was lowering in the sky. "I didn't give up anything."

"Uh-huh." Beau was shaking his head again. "Look at yourself."

"So?" she demanded, opening her arms and looking down at herself, pleased with what she saw. Her silky, dark brown hair was pin-straight past her shoulders—she had her blowout down to a science. She knew her Dior mascara was perfect, because she'd slept on it before and it had still maintained its curl. She had chosen this particular pair of Lucky jeans because they hugged her tennis-toned legs.

But she knew that wasn't what Beau was getting at. What he meant was that back in the day, she would have been rocking matching ratty Converse and a ratty sweatshirt, the better to look like a homeless person.

Oddly, not a look she was all that thrilled to remember.

"You look like you belong in a magazine," Beau said, and it wasn't a compliment. "All *glossy*. I can't even imagine how long it takes you to get dressed in the morning, to make yourself look like that."

Something cold bloomed between Lila's shoulders and slid its way down her spine. While Lila knew for a fact that Carly just rolled out of bed three minutes before homeroom looking perfectly adorable, she, on the other hand, had to get up pretty early to prepare the Lila Beckwith she wanted everyone to see. Sometimes it was exhausting, but she still did it, because she had to.

"And the only thing I've heard you talk about in the past three years is your boyfriend and how popular you are." He made a derisive noise. His eyes were on the road. He wouldn't even look at her when he said it. "But the funny thing is, I don't think you actually *like* your supposedly cool new friends, do you? Because you never look happy. Not the way you used to."

Lila gave him a cool look. "Let's get real, Beau," she suggested mildly enough. "You probably spend just as much time on your careless hipster costumes as I do on looking normal, and we both know you go out of your way to act like you're allergic to the very *hint* of popularity of any kind. Which takes a whole lot more energy than just . . . hanging out with people."

"That's what you call your *mission* to be best friends with Carly Hollander?" Beau asked, laughing slightly. "'Just hanging out'? What about the part where you had to completely turn your back on the person you'd been for your whole life in order to get her to be your friend?"

"She *is* my friend," Lila said quietly.

"Yeah, now," Beau said. He braked, letting the car roll to a stop at a red light. He turned to look at her, his blue eyes dark in the suddenly way-too-close interior of the car. "Once you completely changed. What was wrong with you before?"

Lila didn't know how to answer that. How could she tell him that *everything* was wrong with who she'd been? How could she tell him that, when he'd been such a huge part of it?

The more Beau had disappeared into himself and his misery over his family, the more she'd felt alone. She hadn't really had him anymore—he'd been too angry and too closed off. So she hadn't had anything. She'd wanted more. And once she'd started wanting more, she saw what she had—and who she was—in a brand-new, highly unflattering light.

Suddenly, he leaned toward her.

"What . . . ?" She flinched away in surprise.

But he was only rummaging in the backseat. He pulled a hoodie from the rubble on the floor behind him and shrugged into it.

"Just a little cold," he murmured, sliding an amused look Lila's way. "Relax."

Lila ignored him. Her attention was on the backseat. "You have another guitar?" she asked, incredulous. It was nestled by the back passenger seat, in a case on the floor. Lila was surprised the guitar didn't have a blanket wrapped around it, the way he usually babied his instruments.

"It's my backup," he said.

"You have a backup guitar, which you keep in your car," she said. She laughed. "Wow. So you're, like, a traveling minstrel or something?"

Beau threw her another unreadable look as the light changed from red to green. She braced herself for one of his zingers.

"You never know when you might need a guitar," he said, in such a matter-of-fact way that Lila bit back her next sarcastic comment. What did she know? Maybe in Beau's world, he was often called upon to leap out of his Ford Escort and serenade people with his music.

She was trying to keep from snickering at that mental image when Beau pulled into the Simi Valley train station parking lot. The station looked identical to the last one, and Lila had a strange and unpleasant sense of déjà vu. She snuck a quick peek at her watch: Four seventeen. The train left the station at four twenty-one.

Beau pulled the car into a parking space. Before he'd even opened his door, Lila was out of the car. Her feet flew over the crumbling cement parking lot, and she was aware of Beau's breathing right behind her.

"Which track do you think it's coming in on?" Beau called.

Lila felt like they were on *The Amazing Race* as she shouted back that they'd figure that out inside. She hurled open the surprisingly heavy station doors, narrowly missing a set of suitcases on the floor.

"Come on." Beau grabbed her hand and guided her out to platform three.

They stumbled out into the late-afternoon sunlight. There

was the train, right on the tracks. But it was on its way out of the station. The back window seemed to laugh at them as it disappeared down the track.

Lila watched the flash of silver until the train became a smaller and smaller point in the distance. She slumped against one of the cement platform columns, letting her hair fall down and cover her face.

"This sucks," Beau muttered, his eyes still on what was left of the train.

"I guess we have to keep going," Lila sighed, feeling angry and defeated. *Again.* But there was no time to spare. She straightened, shoved her hair off her face, and pulled the crumpled train schedule from her jeans pocket. "Next stop, Oxnard," she read. "Let's gun it."

"Hold on." Beau pulled his iPhone from his pocket.

"We can't hold on," Lila argued. "We have to hurry!"

"We're not going to catch a train," Beau said, looking up from his phone briefly, the screen reflecting blue on his face. "We can't chase it from station to station—trains are faster than cars, and they don't have to stop."

"So, what?" Lila asked, ignoring the patronizing tone of his statement. She slumped back against the column, annoyed. "What are we supposed to do?"

Beau plucked the schedule from her hand. He frowned at it, then fiddled with his phone, quickly tapping around on the screen. Lila waited as patiently as she could, trying not to bite her nails. Or launch into a screaming fit that would be anything but productive. Though it might make her feel better.

"The train takes seven hours to get up to Oakland," Beau said finally. "But we can drive up the I-5 and be there in like six hours. Five or five and a half, maybe, depending on traffic." He slipped the phone back into his pocket and cocked his head slightly as he looked at her. His shaggy dark hair fell over to one side. "Makes more sense than trying to catch the train at every station, don't you think?"

"Sounds great," Lila said absently. Because what sounded even better was the plan she was quickly outlining in her head. Oakland wasn't too far away from Stanford. After she captured Cooper and beat him to death, she could meet up with Erik. And then she could drive back home with her sweet, attentive, perfect boyfriend, and never have to spend another moment with Beau ever again.

It sounded pretty much like bliss.

8

The I-5 was gridlocked as far as the eye could see. The December sun had started to set, and cars snaked ahead of them, a line of red taillights in the growing darkness. Beau drummed his fingers against the steering wheel, muttered under his breath, and stomped on his brake with more and more force.

"This is ridiculous," he said loudly.

"It's rush hour and it's a holiday," Lila said with an unconcerned shrug. After all, they were only about an hour into the seven hours they had before they caught up with the train in Oakland. "Traffic would be terrible either way, but when you combine them . . ." She let her voice trail off.

Beau glared at her.

"I can't stand traffic," he said. Like it was Lila's fault.

"I don't know how to help you with that," Lila replied, reveling in being the calm one for once.

They inched along, eventually making their way past Magic Mountain and Santa Clarita, then up and over the Grapevine, the stretch of I-5 that snaked into the mountains to the north of the San Fernando Valley and down to the San Joaquin Valley on the other side. Still, the traffic persisted. The 5 was a major highway, but it was only two lanes, and, apparently, the preferred route of many truck drivers. An enormous Mack truck loomed over them, cutting off their vision. Its bumper displayed a cheerful red and yellow sticker asking, *How's My Driving?*. Lila had a feeling, given the way the driver had barricaded them in, that he wasn't overly concerned.

"Screw this," Beau said finally. "I'm taking Route 1."

"Route 1?" Lila stopped pretending to be blithely unconcerned, sat up, and looked at him sharply. "The Pacific Coast Highway is on the coast. We're in the Central Valley." The undertone of her statement was, *duh*.

"Well, now we're headed west toward the water." Beau inched the nose of the Escort forward. They were in the slow lane, and he squeezed his way through a tiny opening, pulling the car into the breakdown lane on the shoulder of the road.

"What the—" Lila's voice was drowned out as the cars around them exploded into an orchestra of honking. She locked eyes with two irate guys in a Lexus and shrugged, sheepishly. Like she had any control—

"Aack!" Lila let out a sudden, unexpected squeal as Beau shifted the Escort into reverse and gunned it. The car shot *backward,* down the road on the narrow shoulder. Hurtling in reverse, Lila felt like she was going to be sick. Finally, Beau hit the brakes and put the car back into drive. He pulled off the gridlocked freeway onto a bumpy, muddy path. It was far more random-farm-path-through-an-orange-grove than back road.

"You're insane," Lila said, twisting around to watch the 5 disappear into the dusk behind the car's taillights. Beau followed the "road" under the freeway and toward the coastal mountains that separated the Central Valley from the ocean and all the famous little beach towns. "Why don't you relax about the traffic? So what if we sit for a while? We have seven hours!"

"We're not sitting in traffic if we don't have to, and we don't have to," Beau said, like that ended the discussion right there. He slammed his foot down on the gas. The old car shuddered in protest and then shot forward, bouncing along the bumpy road.

"Oh, I get it." Lila sniffed, bracing herself against the dashboard. "This is some guy thing."

"It has nothing to do with being a guy," Beau retorted. "It has to do with not wanting to sit in traffic on a road trip that's already a pain in the ass."

Lila opened her mouth to yell back at him, but there was something in the flinty look he shot her that made her think twice. He looked a little too much like the Beau she'd been more than happy to walk away from that day in the cafeteria court-yard, with his nasty *groupie* remark still ringing in her ears. The angry set of his shoulders convinced her that she wouldn't much like that same kind of interaction while she was trapped in a moving car, bumping through someone's crops.

So she stared out the window instead, and tried to concen-trate on the stars that appeared in the twilight sky above the farmland, the ones she could never see at home.

More than an hour later, they were racing up the 1 with the ocean to the left and a practically empty road in front of them. Beau made it over the mountains and down into the sleepy little seaside town of Cambria, then headed north. Even though they'd lost an hour, and Lila's watch told her it was after seven, they hadn't seen much traffic since leaving the 5—a fact Beau had enjoyed pointing out to her. Several times.

The night outside the car was inky black and without any hint of moon, so there was only the winding cliffside road, the sensation of towering trees on one side, and the empty stretch of the ocean on the other.

Lila had always wanted to go to Big Sur, and now she was *in*

Big Sur, and she couldn't see a thing. In fact, she'd seen nothing but Beau for hours.

No wonder she was cranky.

The moment they entered what vaguely resembled a town, Beau pulled the car off the road.

"What are you doing?" Lila asked, sitting up straight and frowning at him.

"I'm hungry," Beau said. He ran a hand over his face tiredly.

"We do *not* have time for some big meal," Lila said, still frowning. Beau could eat enough for an army, and liked to take his time with it, too. Once, he had eaten so much at the local Denny's that the waitress threatened to call the paramedics if he didn't stop. Naturally, Beau had sauntered out without looking like he'd just ingested two orders of cheese fries, Moons Over My Hammy, two Denny's Slamburgers, three milk shakes, and a truckload of hash browns. Lila felt a little queasy at the memory.

"If I'm going to survive this trip," he said, looking at her meaningfully, "I definitely need to keep my energy up."

Beau pulled the car off the road and parked it in a cliffside parking lot. "I'll even buy you something, if you're going to sulk about it," Beau said, smirking.

"I'm not hungry," Lila said through her teeth.

She didn't want whatever Beau might buy her. She would, in fact, rather starve. She fumed as she watched him lope across the parking lot and disappear into the store. Probably, in the grand scheme of things, it didn't really matter that they were stopping for a few minutes. But nice of Beau to consult her! His idea of a compromise was to ignore you until you did things his way. Which most people did, because it wasn't worth the hassle to try to fight with him. That's what Lila had always done—until the day she hadn't.

And he didn't like that very much, she thought with a kind of grim satisfaction. Beau swung back out through the door of the little store, and Lila watched him walk toward her. He had a way of walking like the world owed him something, and he wasn't afraid to hold out for it no matter what. It was a laid-back yet prickly saunter. What if she hadn't stood up for what she wanted back then? How different would things be now? Would they still be together?

Lila shuddered at the idea.

"See?" He climbed back into the car and offered one of his way-too-pleased-with-himself looks her way. Then he tossed a bag of chips and a giant tinfoil-wrapped burrito into the little space between the seats. His version of a snack, which would feed seven people. "That took all of three seconds."

"The train isn't stopping for a snack," Lila pointed out. "I'll be sure to tell your mother that you thought a freaking burrito was more important than your brother."

Beau let out a long-suffering sigh that would have seemed

dramatic for a martyr. Lila made a face but bit her tongue. The last section of this endless day had been, if not exactly *pleasant*, fight-free. Just music playing—Beau had managed to find a mix that didn't involve anything too emo or punk—and the night all around them. It had actually been kind of soothing, the only interruption their periodic attempts to call Amtrak and try to get the train stopped somehow. All they ever got was a recorded *all circuits are busy* message. Eventually, they'd stopped trying.

Lila had zoned out and let herself relax a little bit after the long fall semester and the crappiest of days. She didn't want to start fighting with Beau again if she didn't have to. Much better to crank up the music and float the rest of the way to Oakland— and to Erik. It wasn't exactly a peace treaty, but it was the next best thing.

Beau unwrapped his snack and took a gigantic bite. The smell of beans and cheese and warm tortilla filled the car, and Lila's stomach rumbled. Juggling the enormous burrito, he leaned forward and turned the keys in the ignition.

Clink. Clink.

That was the only sound the car made. The engine didn't turn over. It didn't even sputter.

"And, hey, look at that, the crappiest car in California just died," Lila murmured, inspecting her nails. "What a shock." She knew she sounded like an über-wench, and she didn't even care. So much for not fighting with Beau.

Beau threw her an angry glare, then reached under the steering wheel to pop the hood. He climbed out of the car. Heaving a sigh, Lila decided she had no choice but to follow his lead.

"So you know about cars now?" she asked, walking around the front of the car to stand next to him. The wind was colder in Big Sur and the sky was even clearer. A million pinprick stars glittered above them. She wrapped her arms around herself. Beau scowled down at the engine, his hands on his lean hips.

"Don't worry, Lila," he snapped. "If the engine needs an emergency manicure, I'll be sure to let you know."

"Car trouble?"

They both turned at the new voice. A guy in a blue coverall ambled toward them from the gas station.

"I guess so," Beau said. He rocked back on his heels and let the other man lean in for a closer look. "It won't start."

The man looked at Beau, then at Lila, and then turned his attention to the engine. He pulled a flashlight out of his pocket and let its beam dance over what looked, to Lila, like indistinguishable slabs of dirty metal. She bit her lip and checked the time. Seven thirteen.

The guy *humph*ed. He coughed, spit once, and then rocked back on his heels.

"Well, no, it won't start," the mechanic said, clicking off his flashlight and shoving it back in the pocket of his stained overalls. His face was shadowed in the harsh yellow light from the gas station. He squinted at Beau. "You been off-roading in this thing? It's a Ford Escort, son. Not a jeep."

"I might have gotten a little creative here and there," Beau said, the tips of his ears turning slightly pink. He scuffed his black Converse against the asphalt. "But nothing too crazy."

"Your creativity messed this baby up good," the mechanic crowed. He straightened, his eyes jumping from Beau to Lila. "I can fix it. Four hundred bucks and it's yours by tomorrow, around ten."

"What? No!" Lila piped up, shaking her head in disbelief. By tomorrow, Cooper and Tyler would be in Seattle! And Lila might as well kiss her entire life good-bye. It was already after seven— Beau's little *shortcut* was going to ruin everything. "We can't wait until tomorrow! We have to be in Oakland in a few hours!"

The mechanic shrugged, like their travel plans were about as interesting to him as the Escort's grimy engine was to Lila. *Good-bye, life,* she thought. A loud, thumping bass shattered the night around them, then disappeared as a truck rolled past. Lila's face crumpled, and she knew she was seconds away from bursting into tears.

"Slow night," the mechanic said after a moment, considering. "You want it today, I can probably do it."

"You're a lifesaver!" Lila cried. She wanted to kiss his grizzly cheek, or the gross pavement of the parking lot beneath her feet.

"But it'll cost you double," the man continued.

"No problem," Lila said, even though she could probably *buy* Beau's car for that much money. Or, realistically, for much less. Wasn't that why her dad had given her his credit card, with all those dire warnings about emergencies only and blah blah blah? If this wasn't an emergency, what was?

"It's fine," she said to Beau's pale, questioning face. "I have a credit card."

"That'll have to be cash only," the mechanic said. He shook his head and blew out his cheeks, as if he regretted the necessity.

Lila felt her mouth drop open, but no sound emerged.

"Thanks," Beau said, smiling politely at the mechanic. "If we can just talk for a minute . . . ?"

"No worries," the other man said. "But let me know what you decide in the next ten minutes or so, 'cause I might close down and get some dinner."

"Sure," Beau said weakly.

The man walked away. Beau and Lila stared at each other. Somewhere in the dark, Lila could hear waves crashing against the rocky shore below, again and again.

"You have a credit card?" Beau asked.

"It's my dad's, obviously," Lila said. "For emergencies or whatever."

"Okay." Beau shrugged. "But how would you explain an

eight-hundred-dollar charge in Big Sur if the point is never to tell them about any of this?"

Lila blinked. She hadn't even considered that. "Whatever," she said after a moment, not wanting to admit her mistake. "The real question is, how are we going to come up with eight hundred dollars in cash in the middle of nowhere?"

"We could be in the middle of Hollywood Boulevard and I *still* have no idea how we'd come up with that much money." Beau sighed. He wandered over to the curb and sank down on it. Lila found herself trailing after him. For a moment they just sat there, dejected.

There was only the sound of the wind through the towering pine trees. The clouds scudded across the night sky far above. The air smelled clean and sharp and piney, like salt and Christmas. Lila hugged her knees to her chest and tried to imagine how she would even *start* to have the inevitable conversation with her parents. *Don't worry, I didn't throw a party,* she could say. *But don't get too excited—Cooper is on a train to the North Pole. Not alone! With Tyler!*

Nausea settled in her belly. The hands on her watch seemed to speed up, tick-tocking their way toward her doom. Seven twenty-three. Seven twenty-four. Seven twenty-five.

"I guess we have to call the police," Lila said with a heavy sigh. "Right? I mean, we can't catch the train. And we can't let them go to Alaska or wherever they're headed." She rubbed at her temples. She couldn't even bring herself to imagine what this would mean for her life. Or for her mythical car. "My parents are going to kill me," she whispered, more to herself than to Beau.

"My mom won't love this either," he said darkly. "Believe me."

He fished his phone out of his pocket and looked at it, then made a scoffing sound.

"What?" Lila asked. She felt a sudden surge of hope. "Did they text again?"

"Well, they could have," Beau said in a clipped voice. "I wouldn't know." He held the phone up so Lila could see. "No service."

"Of course not," Lila said, her voice tight. "Why should there be cell phone service? Why should *anything* about this day be *anything* but horrifying?"

"This is happening to both of us, you know," Beau said, his blue eyes narrowing. "Not just you."

Lila was more than ready to unload the entire terrible day's worth of frustration and fury all over him. But she was stopped by the sound of yelling from nearby.

Who could possibly be *more* angry than she was? She twisted around, trying to locate the source of all that fury.

"What do you mean you can't make it?" a man was howling into the pay phone attached to the wall of the convenience store. "You're the *wedding band*! You *have* to make it!"

Beau and Lila stared at each other for a moment. They had exchanged nothing more than not-so-pleasant pleasantries for the last three years, and yet she knew exactly what he was thinking.

He jumped to his feet and walked over to the man just as he slammed the phone down and started shouting curses into the night.

"You need a musician tonight?" he asked, not bothering to conceal his eavesdropping.

"I need a freaking musician *right now*!" the guy retorted, sounding anguished. He was small and round and bald, like an angry bowling ball. He rubbed his fists against his forehead and groaned, his too-large navy blue suit jacket gaping open. The interior panels were a shockingly bright purple paisley. He also happened to be wearing shorts. "I'm the best man for my buddy's wedding, and of course *I* was in charge of the band."

Beau smiled. "If you have eight hundred bucks, I have a guitar and an amp in my car."

"You have to be kidding me," the guy said in a near whisper, clasping his hands together like Beau was the answer to a silent prayer.

"Nope." Beau ambled back to the Escort and pulled out his guitar. "Tell me what you need, and I'm yours."

"You are saving my life!" the guy cried, whooping with joy. He actually jumped up and down in a kind of victory dance.

Beau glanced over at Lila, his brows raised. Once again, she could read his mind: He was remembering her teasing him about his backup guitar.

She was going to hear *all* about that, she was sure.

But maybe this time, she wouldn't mind.

9

CAMP ON A CLIFF
BIG SUR, CA
DECEMBER 22
7:55 P.M.

Camp on a Cliff was spread out across a little bluff that was, true to its name, right on the cliffs overlooking the ocean far below. The wedding party was still eating their dinner on long red picnic tables as Lila and Beau walked up. Candles flickered in hanging lanterns and in votives scattered across the table-tops, and voices wove together in laughter and the clink of glasses. Bright sparkling Christmas lights were strung up in all the trees surrounding dark, green-roofed cabins. Lila wondered if the place looked half as magical during the day, and decided it couldn't. But in the dark, it seemed enchanted.

So enchanted that she found herself smiling at Beau.

So enchanted that he smiled back.

Lila hung near him as he unpacked his guitar and started setting up on the little stage near one of the wood cabins. She leaned back against the rough pine of the cabin wall and watched the wedding reception in front of her. It was, unsurprisingly, a hippie kind of wedding. Who else would get married at a campsite? But Lila had to admit that it all seemed to work. The bride wore a medieval headdress and a red gown, and the groom had a bushy beard and wore stockings like Heath Ledger in *A Knight's Tale*, one of Lila's favorite old-school movies. The groom, sadly, did not otherwise look at all like Heath. The guests were dressed in a riot of colors, with equally surprising hair. Ordinarily, Lila would have thought they were all a bunch of freaks. And it wasn't that she *didn't* think so now, but . . . it all kind of made sense out on this bluff, under the tall trees, in the night air.

"Want to sing with me?" Beau asked as he strummed a few chords. He looked at her from under the messy length of his jet-black hair, then back down at the guitar.

Lila had a sudden, crystal-clear memory of singing with him, of their voices blending together into that harmony that only the two of them could produce—so seamless, she'd thought then. They'd spent their Friday nights cloistered together in his room, composing their silly songs and teaching themselves how to play their guitars.

And then she remembered the day she'd broken up with him in the ninth grade, and all the horrible things they'd said to each other. Like that California would fall into the sea before Lila would sing with Beau again—something, he'd retorted spitefully, he was in no rush for. She had made the right decision back then. She had no doubts. None at all.

So she shook her head slightly, surprised to feel a heat creep across her cheeks as she did.

She was even more surprised a little while later, when Beau started to sing. Lila stood against one of the wood cabins, feeling the rough wood scratch at her back. He had been set up with a chair, his guitar resting comfortably on his knee, a mic before him. He commanded the stage, his biceps peeking out from under his thin T-shirt. It was like he was suddenly the only person alive in the world.

Everyone looks good on a stage, with a guitar, Lila told herself. It was why famous musicians were always considered hot, even when they obviously weren't, and would be ignored on a street corner.

Beau fielded requests from the crowd and sang and played while the bride and groom led the dancing in front of him. He was a big hit—the guests cheered and sang along, and no one sat down.

Lila stood to the side and felt like she was tipping over, falling headfirst into something she didn't understand, as his slightly scratchy voice managed to make old songs sound new. She didn't know how he did it—it was like his voice was a spell, and she was falling under it yet again.

It's just a memory, she told herself sternly. A memory of so many other times she'd watched Beau sing, watched his clever fingers dance across the guitar strings while his voice hinted at poetry and connected with her heart. She felt a tug deep inside her. *Just a leftover memory.*

She looked up and spotted a cluster of girls by the edge of the stage. They had to be *at least* twenty-two, and were eyeing Beau with way too much interest. She tore her gaze away from them and tried to see what they saw when they looked at him.

It wasn't hard to see. Beau's blue eyes seemed to glow against all his dark hair, and his careless T-shirt and jeans showed off his lean, hard body. Lila was forced to admit something she'd been actively denying for years: Beau was hot. One of the best-looking guys she'd ever seen, as a matter of fact. It probably would have gone to someone else's head. But Beau was always, defiantly, Beau.

He wasn't as big as Erik, and he definitely didn't work out, or walk around with Erik's adorable cockiness. But there was something about the way Beau held himself that made it clear he wasn't to be messed with. That he belonged up on a stage, in front of a crowd, always and forever on his own terms.

Just then, he looked right at her and smiled.

"And now for something a little lighter," he said into the microphone. He still held Lila's gaze. He strummed a chord, then another.

No way.

Lila knew those chords as well as she'd once known Beau. He'd written the song to cheer her up when she had a cold in the seventh grade. The next time he sang it was over the phone, while she was visiting her relatives in Michigan the summer after eighth grade. They'd dubbed it their lullaby. They'd added to the song over the years, and sung it to and with each other ever since. Up until ninth grade, anyway. Lila remembered every single word.

"Roses are red, violets are blue, are you allergic to flowers, too?" Beau sang now, up onstage. The dim light from above bounced off his cheekbones. *"What if I brought you cookies instead? One sniff of your roses and I could be dead."*

Lila smiled back at him. But she still didn't get up to join him at the mic.

It was one thing to appreciate the past. It was something else to relive it.

"That guy was lying through his teeth," Beau said as he eased back into his Ford Escort a couple hours later. He settled himself in the driver's seat and glared through the windshield at the blue-coveralled mechanic, who had the nerve to wave at them.

"About what?" Lila asked quietly, suddenly feeling oddly shy

in Beau's company. Probably because she was tired. It had been
the longest day of her life.

"The car wasn't *that* jacked up," Beau said. "He said it was
done hours ago."

"But I'm betting he took all the money anyway." Lila's dad
had pointed out on many occasions that mechanics were all
crooks—all the more reason she should appreciate not having
a car.

"I talked him down, but it was still six hundred and fifty,"
Beau said ruefully. "My best-paying gig ever, and I spent most
of the money on this damn car."

Probably his best-received gig, too, Lila thought as he guided
the Escort out of the gas station parking lot and back to the
winding seaside road. The guests had crowded around him at
the end of the reception, and more than one had asked for his
phone number, claiming they had parties they wanted him to
play, all over the state of California. One woman claimed she
would fly him to Iowa. *Cougar.*

"Here," Beau said, snapping Lila out of her thoughts. She had
moved on to a happy fantasy where she told all the old women
exactly how little chance they had with Beau. He hated everybody. He certainly wouldn't go for the elderly!

He tossed his iPhone at her, and she caught it by reflex. She
blinked down at it.

"Check to see when we get service," he said. "We have to

figure out how far behind the train we are. It's going to suck if they made it to Canada or something while we were trying to get out of Big Sur."

Oh, right. *Reality.* Lila wasn't hanging out with Beau to hear him sing or to remember that time back when or to watch old ladies slobber all over him. Or even to come to terms with his good looks. She was on a mission to retrieve Cooper and save herself from a lifetime grounding. She scowled down at the phone.

Ten minutes out from the convenience store, Lila squealed in delight.

"Service!" she cried.

"Excellent," Beau said with relief. "And about freaking time."

Lila laughed a little as she went online and quickly looked up the status of the train on the Amtrak website. She drew in a quick breath.

"Let me guess," Beau said. "It turned supersonic and is now in Vancouver. Because why not, after everything else tonight?"

"No," Lila said, still not believing it herself. She waved the iPhone at him, as if he could read it while navigating the dark, treacherous road. "It's been delayed! It's been sitting on the track outside San Luis Obispo for a couple of hours already!"

"No way," Beau said, laughing. He turned toward Lila, a happy glint in his eyes. "You mean we're actually getting some good luck?"

"There's a scheduled crew change in San Jose," Lila read off the Amtrak site as she scrolled down further. "We can intercept them there, instead of in Oakland."

"Perfect," he said immediately, and grinned at her.

She returned his smile and settled back in her seat. Maybe it wouldn't be the worst thing in the world to spend some more time in the car with Beau.

10

SAN JOSE AMTRAK STATION
SAN JOSE, CA
DECEMBER 23
12:33 A.M.

Gritty-eyed and jacked up on way too much roadside coffee—with a generous helping of SweeTarts and Cool Ranch Doritos—Lila was more than ready to collar Cooper and throw him in the back of the car when Beau pulled into the San Jose train station.

"The train is still about seven minutes out," Beau said after he parked the car, glancing at his phone.

"Check it out." Lila climbed out into the chilly night air, stretching her cramped limbs. "We can actually *walk* into the station and figure out which track the train is supposed to arrive on. It's like we're on vacation or something." She barely noticed the cold, thanks to the adrenaline pumping through her veins. She pulled her leather jacket tighter around her and shoved her hands into her pockets. The air smelled like gasoline and something sickly sweet and floral—a far cry from the clean seaside air in Big Sur.

Beau grinned across the hood of the Escort and pulled his hunter green sweatshirt up close around his head. The wind picked up and seemed to blow right through them as they stood there. It had been getting steadily colder as they traveled north. It almost felt the way Lila supposed December *should* feel.

"It's freezing up here," Beau said, blowing on his hands. He started for the old train station's doors. As Lila followed, she found herself focusing on the strangest things: the way the cuffs of Beau's jeans were frayed and dragged against the ground. The way he leaned slightly against the cold as he walked. The way his jeans hugged his— She shook her head a little bit and snuggled deeper into her hot pink scarf. The caffeine and sugar had clearly addled her brain.

Inside the station, the lights were so bright they were almost dizzying. Lila had to blink a few times to see clearly. She frowned, looking up at the board and trying to make sense of all the arrivals and departures.

"This way," Beau said. He motioned with his elbow, his hands shoved into his pockets. Lila walked beside him toward the track, wondering idly if the people who saw them together thought they were a couple.

As they passed a glass window, she looked at their reflection. While Beau's scruffiness was downplayed by his surprisingly nice hoodie, her own trademarked put-together-ness had taken a serious hit. She'd been forced to pile the entire mass of her carefully blown-out dark hair on top of her head, using an elastic she'd found in Beau's glove compartment. She chose not to wonder who the elastic might have belonged to in its previous life. She looked bedraggled and crazy-eyed from all the coffee and sweets. If anyone *did* think she and Beau were together, they would no doubt be wondering how such a hot mess had snagged such a sexy guy.

"Crap," Beau muttered.

"Crap?" she echoed.

"I think we have to have tickets to board the train." Beau nodded toward the entrance to the track, where a uniformed employee stood guard.

"Why can't we just get on, grab them, and get off?" Lila asked.

"If you want to argue with that guy, go right ahead," Beau said. Lila took a closer look at the uniformed guard. He was radiating unfriendliness even from a distance, like Dwight on *The Office*. He looked like he would welcome the opportunity to ruin someone else's Friday night. Lila sighed.

"Yeah," Beau said. "I'll buy us tickets."

"You're using the leftover money from Big Sur, right?" Lila asked, suddenly afraid that he was using his own money. Lila was fine with him using *that* money, but she didn't want him to use his own to fund a caper that had probably been Cooper's idea.

Beau shook his head at her, his mouth curving slightly, like he had just tracked every thought that crossed her mind.

"Stay right here," he said quietly.

A few minutes later he was back, tickets in hand. He presented them to Mr. Surly at the gate. Lila walked behind him, checking her watch. Twelve thirty-five. The train was due at 12:40.

"How should we do this?" Lila asked, peering down the track, her stomach tightening in anticipation as she saw the point of light in the distance that heralded the arrival of the long-overdue train. "How do we find them before the train leaves again?"

"I figure you start at one end and I'll start at the other," Beau said. "Meet in the middle when we're done." The train whistle sounded, forcing him to raise his voice as the train whooshed into the station and the PA crackled to life above them. "Make sure you check the bathrooms!" He took off running, chasing the front of the train down the track.

Lila moved in the opposite direction, headed for the last car. Once the train stopped, she swung aboard, not even waiting for any of the passengers to exit.

"Excuse *me!*" huffed one affronted lady, but Lila had much bigger fish to fry. Like her brother, who she'd happily fry the second she got her hands on his grimy green sweatshirt.

The train was much longer than Lila had expected it to be—not that she'd previously given much thought to the length of trains, or for that matter trains at all, unless it was for one of those boring SAT math questions. She moved through the cars swiftly, on a mission, scanning the seats and looking in each bathroom or pounding on the locked door until the person inside angrily proved they weren't Cooper. In one car, she saw a flash of green and messy brown hair poking over a seat. *Gotcha*, she thought. She threw herself at the seat, only to find herself face-to-face to with a startled mother and a little girl who definitely wasn't Cooper.

"Um, sorry," Lila mumbled, and kept moving.

It wasn't until she was almost to the middle of the train that she started to panic.

Where is he?

For the first time, her own annoyance and anger over her foiled plans faded away, and Lila was confronted with the fact that her eight-year-old brother was hours away from home. And not where she'd imagined him to be. Her heart began to pound. He was obnoxious, sure, but he was still her brother. He had the street smarts of a fluffy bunny. She wanted to kill him, but she didn't actually want anything to *happen* to him.

"He has to be here!" she said out loud, desperately, startling the couple in the seats directly in front of her. She forced a smile and kept going.

Above her, the intercom crackled, and the conductor warned that the train was preparing to leave the station. Lila panicked. What if something really had happened to Cooper? Her panic rising in her throat, she moved even faster, bursting through the doors into the middle car—the snack car.

"All people not traveling on this service, please exit the train immediately," the conductor droned from the speakers up above.

Lila looked around frantically at the makeshift café and long, empty tables. She glanced up to see Beau charging in through the doors at the other end of the car, his forehead wrinkled into a fierce frown, his hands empty.

"How can this be happening?" Lila demanded, knowing perfectly well he didn't know any better than she did. "Beau— where are they?"

"Maybe they're holed up somewhere," he said, sounding desperate. "We ran through the train—maybe we didn't look as closely as we could have."

There was a lurch, and then the train began to roll.

"Great," Lila said in despair, twisting to look out the window.

"We'll look again," Beau said grimly. "We'll—"

"Beau."

He stopped talking, and followed the finger she pointed out the windows, to the platform beyond.

Cooper and Tyler stood there, shoulder to shoulder, sporting identical smug grins. The two boys waved excitedly as the train picked up speed. It hurtled forward, taking Beau and Lila with it, away from the platform.

And farther and farther away from their brothers.

11

Fifty-three minutes later, their tempers at a low yet consistent throb, Lila and Beau climbed off the train they'd never wanted to board in the first place and found themselves in Oakland.

In the middle of the night.

Without either of their brothers, or Beau's car.

Lila had spent the train ride calling and texting Erik from Beau's phone with zero success. She finally gave up and let Beau try to reach their brothers. So much for the big go-to-Stanford-and-abandon-Beau plan. Or for the *screw your final and go catch my brother at the San Jose train station and keep him in a headlock* addition.

Beau looked up from his phone, catching Lila's gaze. "We're screwed. They still aren't picking up."

"I see you've mastered the power of positive thinking," Lila muttered, even though she actually agreed with him. She pulled the elastic out of her hair and attempted to tame her locks into a neater ponytail. They were now an hour from Beau's car—and their horrible little brothers. Assuming, of course, that Cooper and Tyler had stayed put. For all Lila knew, they could be on their way to Timbuktu at this point. By raft.

"And Erik's a dead end?" Beau asked.

"What's that supposed to mean?" she demanded, a defensive spark skittering up her spine.

Beau blinked. "I mean, he didn't answer his phone when you called, right?"

Fluorescent lights buzzed softly overhead. Someone had scratched the initials *KZ + JM* into one of the station's glass walls. Lila tugged on her new ponytail and scowled at him. "Like I told you on the train, he has a major take-home final due tomorrow. So yeah, it'd be awesome if he could come pick us up, but the truth is, I'd be shocked if he answered his phone. He's probably holed up in the library, working his ass off. He's really determined to get great grades this semester, which takes a whole lot of dedication and work—I mean, he was obviously going to come to my party until he found out about this exam. . . ."

A man in the corner with a gray mustache rustled his copy of the *Oakland Tribune*. Beau was staring at her, his eyes bluer than ever in the canary yellow lighting. The expression in them wasn't mocking or superior—just weary.

Which for some reason made her feel even more defensive.

"Even if he has his phone with him at the library," Lila continued, knowing she was rambling but unable to stop the word vomit, "And even if it's turned on at this point, why would he answer? He probably doesn't answer unfamiliar numbers, and obviously he doesn't know yours. Why would he? It's not like you and he have ever even spoken a sentence to each other, much less been, like, phone buddies!"

Beau held up a finger to silence her. "I have an idea," he said in his careful tone, the one Lila had always hated. He handed her his phone. "You stay here and keep trying. I'm going to go over there"—he pointed across the station toward the information booth—"and see about getting a train back to San Jose, so we can at least have a car while we figure out our next move. Okay?"

"Fine, but I'm telling you, he won't pick up," Lila said. Mustache Man folded up the paper and dropped it in a trash can, frowning at a straggler who was passed out on a long wood bench. "He probably thinks somebody from my party is drunk-dialing him."

She envisioned Erik, hunched over a table in the library, surrounded by towers of dusty books. In her fantasy, he was even wearing glasses, looking incredibly scholarly and cute. He would glance at the number that kept flashing on his cell phone screen, but of course he was *far* too busy to engage in a conversation in the middle of an exam.

Lila ignored the niggling voice in the back of her mind telling that he wasn't responding to her texts, either. But maybe he'd just finished his take-home final a little early and crashed. Why stay up when he was finished? And why leave the ringer on when he was desperate for a good night's sleep?

She opened her mouth to point that out, but Beau just shrugged and started for the booth. Lila glared at his retreating back and wrapped her scarf in a tighter knot around her neck, punching in Erik's number once again.

The phone rang and rang, until Erik's voice came on the line: *Hey, this is Erik. Leave me a message and I'll hit you back.* Lila hung up, feeling like hitting something herself. Surely a truly perfect boyfriend would be able to sense, somehow, that she was stranded a zillion miles from home, right? That she was having a sibling emergency of the worst kind. Even if he was at the library, or asleep?

But Erik's perfect-boyfriend sensor was clearly on the fritz, because he failed to pick up the next three times she tried, one right after the other—like the clingy, needy, high school girlfriend she had always prided herself on never being.

"I told you," she said matter-of-factly when Beau walked back to her side and looked at her expectantly. "He's taking an exam."

Beau rocked back a little in his Converse sneakers and shrugged. "There are no more trains back to San Jose tonight."

"Crap." Lila rubbed at her temples. "Okay, what do we do?"

"The way I see it, we have two options," Beau said. He stuffed his hands in the pockets of his jeans and shook his shaggy hair out of his face. "Number one, we sleep here, on the floor."

"Pass," Lila said immediately, wrinkling her nose at the sticky linoleum tiles. They were covered with suspicious-looking brown splotches.

"I figured as much." He studied her face for a moment. "Option number two is we cab it to Stanford and find Erik. Borrowing his car will be faster than waiting until tomorrow morning for the next train."

"Done," Lila said at once. She frowned at him. "Wait. Why did you present that like it was a bad option?"

Beau heaved a sigh and nodded toward the station's doors. "Do you want to find a cab or stand here talking about how great your missing boyfriend is?"

Fuming, Lila brushed past him and headed for the doors. Suddenly, she was desperate to see Erik, to remind herself what a great guy looked like.

The cab reached Palm Drive, the palm tree–lined stretch that served as the entrance to Stanford, at exactly 2:12 a.m.

Even though she was exhausted, Lila marveled at the lush oval great lawn and the graceful stone buildings that stood sentinel over it.

She climbed out of the cab, leaving Beau to pay the driver, and took a moment to drink in her dream campus. Since she was a little kid, the word *college* had evoked images of Stanford—the red-roofed buildings, the colorful façade of Memorial Church, the rolling foothills that loomed in the distance. Tonight, students in small groups wandered across the wide lawns and walkways, heading to and from parties. Their laughter and shouts cut through the darkness, making Lila's whole body tingle in anticipation. Suddenly, she knew that everything was going to be okay.

"So . . . where do we look first?" Beau asked, coming up behind her. The cab picked up a pair of drunk boys dressed in eighties gear and sped off. "Any idea where he'd be?"

His tone sounded the opposite of thrilled, like of all the mishaps they'd endured tonight, this was a particularly excruciating chore. For him, it probably was. She thought of what he'd said back in ninth grade, after he'd found out Lila was dating Erik. *I'm sure you two will have a lot to talk about,* he'd sneered. *Like Erik, Erik, and, oh yeah, more Erik.*

"Of course I know where he'll be," she said loftily, and quickly led Beau down the path to the Green Library. The building soared above the quad, red-roofed and graceful, practically daring you to come inside and learn.

Lila opened the door to the side entrance Erik had showed her when she'd visited in October, then wove her way through the labyrinth of bookshelves and study carrels. It didn't take long to find Erik's favorite study spot, hidden away in a corner of a special collections room.

It was empty.

"That's weird," Lila said, frowning at the wood desk.

"Maybe he's sitting somewhere else," Beau suggested. "This place is huge." He turned on his heel and started down a different aisle.

Lila trailed after Beau, supposedly searching for Erik, but her heart wasn't in it. He had told Lila a million times that he did all his work in that nook, and Erik was a guy who liked his habits. Meaning . . . if he wasn't in his usual spot, he wasn't studying.

"Maybe he's back in his dorm room," Lila said, as much to herself as to Beau, when they walked back out of the library.

"Yeah, you're probably right." Beau nodded all too agreeably.

Lila hitched her purse higher on her shoulder, not trusting the casualness of Beau's words.

They walked in silence across the library's lawn over to the main quad, where Erik's all-freshman residence hall was located.

A boy in a Santa hat and boxers let them into the building.

Lila had to stop herself from running up the poured concrete steps to Erik's room on the fourth floor.

When they reached 4C, Lila elbowed Beau out of the way. "Let me do the talking." She pounded on his door for a full minute, but there was no answer.

Beau cocked an eyebrow. "Try the door," he suggested.

"And totally violate his privacy?" Lila huffed, hands on hips. Cool girlfriends did *not* storm their boyfriends' rooms in the middle of the night. Well, unless a make-out session was involved.

Beau just tapped his watch, then turned the metal door handle.

The door swung open noiselessly. Beau lounged in the doorway while Lila walked inside and stood for a moment, breathing in the emptiness. There was a light on next to Erik's bed, his laptop closed up tight on his desk. The window was open, and there was a duffel bag on the floor, but no clue as to Erik's whereabouts. She could feel Beau's eyes watching her.

He wasn't in the library. He wasn't in his room.

Lila was forced to confront the possibility that she didn't know Erik's every last move the way she thought she did. And she could tell by the way Beau was flaring his nostrils that he'd reached the same conclusion. A rush of irrational anger coursed through her veins—at Erik for vanishing into thin air but, even more, at Beau for witnessing it.

"What are we going to do?" she asked, sinking down on the bed as calmly as possible. Her throat felt tight, and her left leg was shaking the way it always did when she was on the verge of hysteria. "I have no idea where he is."

The strains of a Kanye song floated through Erik's window, followed by a loud crash and a high-pitched giggle.

"Sounds like someone is having a serious party," Beau said, ignoring her question and—thankfully—her glassy eyes. He crossed the room and stuck his head out the window. "I think it's just one floor down."

"Well, I'm glad someone's having fun," she muttered as the new JT hit started blaring. She thought briefly of all her friends at Yoon's party, taking pictures, playing Beirut, and probably laughing about how poor Lila got grounded because of her loser brother.

"Come on," Beau said, standing up and jerking his chin toward the door. He was grinning.

"Huh?" She blinked up at him.

"Weren't you supposed to be at a party tonight?" he asked. "So what if this one is three hundred and fifty miles away from the one you planned?"

Lila shook her head but got up. She and Beau followed the noise downstairs until they found themselves on the edge of a huge party spilling out from a set of rooms along the third floor hallway. Everywhere Lila looked, happy Stanford students drank from red plastic cups, laughed with their friends, or danced on blond wood desks.

Naturally, Beau dove right into the chaos.

Lila reached out and grabbed the back of his hoodie, which didn't exactly stop him in his tracks. Instead, she somehow found herself moving through the throngs to keep up with him.

"What are you doing?" she demanded.

"This is a party, Lila." He glanced back at her, smirking a bit. "Surely *you* of all people know how to party."

"Very funny," she said, having to lean closer and raise her voice over the music. "We are not here to party. We are here to find Erik, get his car, and stop our moronic brothers before they actually make it to the North Pole!"

"Yes," Beau said, turning to face her. Her hand dropped away from his sweatshirt. The smirk left his lips, his eyes suddenly serious as they met hers. "But we don't even know what train they're on at this point."

"Beau, we don't—" Lila began.

"Lila." The way he said her name made her go quiet. Or maybe it was how the light bouncing off the haphazardly strung-up disco ball made his eyes seem oddly hypnotic.

"Cooper and Tyler—"

"—are probably being fussed over by some sweet Amtrak

worker right now," Beau said. "They have a phone. They'll call if they need us. And how far can they get tonight?"

"I don't know," she said. A lump lodged itself in the back of her throat. She swallowed hard. A group of kids in the hall were chanting, "Chug, chug, chug!"

"Breathe," he instructed. "We've had a very long, very stressful day. We've been hitting our heads against walls all night. Let's relax for a few minutes—regroup. Maybe taking a second for ourselves will help."

She let his words sink in, and just like that, the lump evaporated. Maybe Beau was right. How much more defeat could she handle tonight anyway?

Why *not* enjoy an illicit Stanford party?

"Atta girl." Beau angled her around a couple far too busy crawling all over each other to move aside, and snagged them two Cokes before finding wall space to lean against.

"Not exactly party material," Lila teased him, waving her can of Coke at him. A girl next to her swayed on four-inch heels. The couple in the corner continued to grope each other.

"Well, as much as I want to do a keg stand with all the frat boys," Beau replied with an exaggerated sigh, "I do have to drive later, so—"

"Bummer." She laughed and cracked open her can. Already she could feel the tension leaving her body. "I know how much you love keg stands."

"It's a seriously underappreciated art form," Beau dead-panned.

Lila took a long pull of her lukewarm soda and watched in amazement as a red-faced boy staggered down the hall and tripped over his own feet. He plowed, face-first, into what was once a coffee table, crumpling it beneath his weight as he fell.

"So this is what you wanted to do to your parents' house?" Beau leaned back against the wall and smiled slightly, like the chaos pounding around them was a movie he was watching. Lila studied him for a second. He looked out of place in the crowd of prepsters, but it wasn't just his clothes. Beau stood differently than the other guys. More sure on his feet, somehow. And Lila had a feeling it wasn't just because he was sober.

"Please," Lila said breezily. "I wasn't throwing a *frat* party!"

"Ah, yes. Because high school parties are way more refined," Beau said. Teasing her, she realized as he grinned down at her. Not provoking. Just teasing.

"My parties, by definition, are the classiest high school parties in Southern California," she told him grandly. "Or would be, if I could throw one without Cooper ruining everything."

"You know, *classy* and *high school party* are not terms you often find in the same sentence."

"You are such a snob," she told him.

He let out a bark of laughter. "How can you even say that with a straight face?" he asked, grinning at her. "Seriously."

Lila tried to frown, but her lips curved up in a grin instead. She'd forgotten how well they did the light, fun banter thing.

The room had gotten even more crowded, and now Beau was standing just inches from Lila. His whole body was angled toward her, his arm brushing against her shoulder.

Just then, the make-out couple finally broke apart for some air, and the girl began dancing. "I love this song!" she shrieked, moving her hips to the driving beat.

The girl's make-out partner locked his arms around her waist from behind. Lila saw the spray of freckles on his neck, first—the ones that almost exactly replicated the Big Dipper. Then she saw the sloppy, sexy smile he directed at the girl who shimmied in front of him. Finally, she saw the way he cocked his head so that his blond hair flopped a little bit to the side, like a little boy's.

Lila's stomach dropped through her feet and smacked into the floor. Her mouth fell open. Time stopped.

It was Erik.

12

Lila staggered out of the heavy dormitory doors. She sucked in a breath, then another, but still felt like she couldn't breathe. Like there was a giant hand wrapped around her ribs, crushing her. She looked around wildly, unable to get her bearings. She could hardly believe what she'd seen, even though she'd seen it with her own eyes. Eyes that she would gladly rip out of her head, if it meant she could erase that vision. Her brain kept playing the scene over and over again—the way Erik had kissed the girl, how his hands had traveled down her body . . .

"Stop it!" she hissed at herself. Her stomach roiled, and her breath came fast and shallow. Heat prickled behind her eyes, and she knew that she was seconds away from bursting into tears, crumpling to the ground, and sinking into a gooey mess of despair—

"Lila!"

Beau dashed out of the dorm, the door slamming loudly behind him. It was only then that Lila realized she was moving. Running, actually, putting space between her and that damn party and the sickening realization that Erik wasn't the guy she'd thought he was. That she didn't know him at all—because the Erik *she* knew never would have had his tongue down some random girl's throat at a party he was supposed to be too busy to go to in the first place. Lila felt a sob catch in her throat, and fought it back down. She would *not* cry. Would not break. Would not let her guard down in front of Beau.

But she did stop walking. Leaning against a scratchy palm trunk, she steadied her breathing. The dorm behind them was still pounding out the music. A group of college kids walked by, undoubtedly tipsy, all of them laughing as the guy in the middle told a story that required huge hand gestures.

"I don't want to talk about it," Lila snapped at Beau when he jogged to her side. She crossed her arms tightly over her chest, like it would help her keep everything inside.

"Fine," he told her.

But she could feel his reaction, the judgment vibrating off him like an electric charge, and she hated him for it. She hated Erik for doing this to her, and she hated herself for being so stupid, so gullible, so *trusting*.

"I'm serious!" she cried. A wave of humiliation crashed over her. Her cheeks burned, but her body felt cold and shaky. "Like it isn't bad enough that my boyfriend is cheating on me?" she demanded, as if Beau had said something instead of just quietly judging her. "It has to be in front of you, of all people?" Her voice cracked when she said *you*. Terrific.

"What did you expect?" Beau asked, in a tone completely devoid of anything resembling sympathy. "Erik is a douche."

Lila's mouth fell open. "Excuse me?"

A normal person would comfort a girl who had just witnessed her boyfriend cheating on her, no matter how complicated his relationship with the girl and the boyfriend in question. A gentle *don't cry* pat on the back. A hug, even. But Beau was not normal. He was a sadist. Why offer comfort when he could criticize instead?

"Come *on*, Lila," Beau said, sounding almost impatient. "I'm not saying anything you don't already know. Are you really that surprised?"

He pursed his lips, like he was physically restraining himself from saying *I told you so.* Instantly, she was transported back to that awful conversation outside the cafeteria. She could see his superior sneer, that disappointed yet mocking gleam in his eyes. Could feel her stomach cramp at his contempt.

"Really?" she demanded. They were standing in the middle of the crosswalk, with dark green lawns all around them. She used to dream about walking across these fields with Erik.

"*Really*, Beau? We catch my boyfriend of three years sucking face with some college slut at a frat party and the only thing you can manage to say is that he's a *douche*?"

"What else is there to say?" he asked, pushing his dark hair away from his blue eyes. "It's the unavoidable truth about Erik Hollander."

Lila was so furious her ears were ringing. "What kind of human being are you? Who *says* something like that?"

"You're yelling at *me*?" Beau replied, amazed. "Reality check, Lila. I'm not the guy you're mad at."

The ringing in her ears got even louder, and she opened her mouth to tear into Beau—

But then she realized the ringing was not, in fact, in her head. It was in her pocket. Someone was calling Beau's phone. Lila wasn't sure if she was happy to be interrupted, but she tore the phone out of her pocket anyway and blinked at the damn thing until it made sense.

Lila, read the display.

"Cooper!" Lila cried into the phone. "Where are you?" She was annoyed when Beau moved closer, pushing his head near hers so he could hear too. She wanted to hit him, not cuddle over a phone with him.

"You guys looked so mad!" Cooper crowed. "We figured when the train got delayed that you guys might catch up to us, but we never thought we'd get to *see* you. How awesome was that?"

"Yeah, awesome," Lila said sarcastically. A university cop made his way down the path, eying Lila and Beau suspiciously before moving on. "It's the middle of the night and you're roaming around San Jose by yourself—you, who have night-mares after watching totally not scary movies. Really awesome, Coop."

"We're not in San Jose," Cooper told her, giggling. The unmistakable sound of Tyler's laughter could be heard in the background, egging him on. Beau leaned in even closer. Lila fought the urge to elbow him. Hard. "I told you, we thought you might catch up with us. So when we saw you get on the train, we jumped off. And then the last train of the night came through like ten minutes later! Ha!"

"Ha-ha," Lila said, miserably. "Please tell me you're on the last train of the night heading back to L.A."

"Nope." Cooper laughed again. "Oh, and Mom called."

Lila froze.

"What did she say?" Lila asked, trying to sound calm. She felt Beau shift beside her.

"I told her you were in the shower," Cooper said blithely. "She said they were having fun with Aunt Lucy, and Phoenix is really hot, and she'd see us Sunday night."

Sunday night. The words echoed in Lila's head like a death sentence. "Great," Lila said, pressing her free hand against her forehead and the sudden headache that bloomed there. "And what do you think she's going to do when she gets home and discovers you're on your way to the North Pole, Cooper?"

"Oh, she loves Santa too," Cooper said happily, reminding Lila that no matter how annoying he was, he was still only eight years old. And clearly living in a fantasy world. A fantasy world Lila could shatter with the simple truth about Santa Claus. But something held her back from saying it. Perhaps it was the vision of being grounded for the next seventeen years.

"To *me*, Cooper!" she cried, frustrated. "What do you think she's going to do to *me*?"

But Cooper only giggled some more.

"Sleep tight!" Tyler called in the background, and then the line went dead.

For a moment Lila stood, the phone still to her ear, as if mid-conversation with a reality check. Her party had blown up in her face. Her mission to recover Cooper had failed. Her relationship with Erik was nothing but a lie. And every tick of her watch brought her closer to doom.

Which left her with what, exactly?

"Um, Lila." Beau snapped his fingers in front of her eyes. "You okay?"

"Oh, I'm great," she said, glaring at Beau for all kinds of reasons, starting with the fact that he was right there. "Fan-fricking-tastic."

Beau sighed, and the sound ignited something in Lila.

"Tell you what," she threw at him, so mad her teeth snapped together. "You stay right here and keep *sighing* like that. It's so helpful. I'm going to take a cab to San Jose and get your stupid piece-of-crap Escort. Then I'm going to keep driving after the Santa stalkers."

"Fine," Beau said, his blue eyes narrow. "I can—"

"Alone!" Lila yelled at him. "I'm going *alone*! How about you just go back home and sit in your basement and be as judgy and nasty and angry at the whole world as you want!"

Beau was staring at her like her head had just exploded. She knew she was too loud, and bordering on hysterical.

"Whoa," he said, with infuriating calmness, holding his hands up in surrender.

The gesture made her want to curl into a ball, watch really depressing movies like *Titanic*, and cry for the next three weeks.

Which she couldn't do even if she wanted to, because she had less than twenty-four hours to find Cooper and drag his behind back to L.A. Less than twenty-four hours, if she was realistic. Her parents would likely come home before midnight on Christmas Eve.

"Give me your keys," she snapped at Beau.

"You can't be serious."

She let out a loud groan of frustration. "Beau!"

He reached into his pocket, and pulled out his keys. His eyes searched her face, like there was something he was looking for. Like there was something obvious she was missing.

Lila snatched the keys from his hand. Then she turned away and started marching across the campus. Her heels drummed into the ground as she walked, faster and faster, like she could somehow make things better by putting distance between herself and the latest, worst problem.

But she couldn't deny the emptiness she felt when she looked behind her and saw that Beau wasn't there, like she half-expected him to be. He wasn't following her. He didn't care about her.

He was letting her go.

13

Of course, there were no cabs. Lila didn't know what she'd been thinking. Why would taxis cruise a college campus? It was hard enough to get a taxi in Los Angeles. As she trudged across the campus, Stanford seemed less ideal with each step. Big stone buildings leaned together like whispering friends, mocking her loneliness. Dark, empty lawns mirrored what her life had become. And the clock tower overhead signaled that with every passing second, Cooper was getting farther away—and with him any hope she had of rescuing what remained of her life.

Tick tock, it hissed. *Tomorrow night is getting closer and closer to* tonight *every minute. . . .*

Like she needed the reminder.

Just then, a cab pulled into view and stopped at the curb just a few yards ahead of Lila.

"Thank you!" Lila murmured, sending a little prayer of thanks up to whatever benevolent spirit was finally looking out for her. *More of this, please!* She ran toward the cab while two obviously drunk sorority girls tried to climb out of the car, shrieking with laughter.

A honk sounded from behind. Frowning, Lila twisted around, just as a familiar black Maxima slid into view. Her stomach twisted.

Erik had come for her?

Had he seen her at the party and realized the enormity of what he'd done? Was he about to beg for forgiveness? Beg her to take him back?

And the million-dollar question: Would she?

As the car pulled to a stop, Lila peered inside, expecting to see Erik's blond mop. But the driver had jet-black hair and wore a hoodie.

"Beau?" Confusion washed over her.

"Get in," he said, his gaze connecting with hers.

"I'll get in, cutie!" the drunk girl on the sidewalk called. "Is he cute, Ashley? He sounds cute!"

"He's cute," her friend replied. "But why are you still lying there?" she asked the girl collapsed on the sidewalk with her clutch beside her.

Lila stepped toward the driver's window of Erik's car.

"Isn't this . . . ?" She drifted closer. "This *is* Erik's car, right?"

Beau just looked at her.

"But—"

"I saw his keys when we looked in his room earlier," Beau said, his chin sticking out almost defiantly.

"So you just . . ." She gestured wordlessly at the car.

"I went back and grabbed them," he said. "He deserves to lose his car after what he did to you."

Lila felt a warmth in the pit of her stomach. In a way, he was saying he'd stolen Erik's car for her. It was the sweetest thing she'd heard all night. The irony of that made her want to laugh, or maybe cry.

Beau clearly interpreted her silence as disapproval, because he continued talking, like he was laying out his case.

"Also, we've already lost time," he said. "We'll lose even more time if we have to double back to San Jose to pick up my car. The train isn't going to wait for us."

Lila smiled. "I like the way you think," she said and climbed inside.

There was the familiar leather and pine smell. The usual fuzzy dice hanging from the rearview mirror, which Erik had always claimed were a joke. There was a stack of CDs in the well between the seats, probably classic rock like Journey. It was more than a little strange to be in Erik's car without Erik—not to mention *with* Beau. But then Lila remembered the way Erik had jammed his tongue in that girl's mouth, and decided it wasn't so strange after all.

"I don't know why I'm surprised," she said as Beau guided the Maxima toward the campus exit. "Grand theft auto kind of goes with the whole antisocial, edge-of-society thing you have going on."

He shot her a slight grin before returning his attention to the road. They were the only car on the road, and all the traffic lights were blinking yellow.

"I love that you see me that way," he said. "Especially when it couldn't be further from the truth."

"Are you claiming you're *not* antisocial?" Lila shook her head in mock disbelief.

"There's a difference between being antisocial and just having other stuff on my mind," he pointed out. "It's possible to not care about the latest North Valley High scandal without it being a statement."

"If you say so." Lila looked down at her lap. "Anyway, thank you for stealing a car for me."

Beau laughed softly, hanging a right. "It wasn't just for you. I'm trying to get Tyler back, too, you know."

"Sure," Lila said. Of course Beau wanted to get his little brother home, safe and sound. "But your mom is so much cooler than my parents. She'll forgive you."

There was silence for a moment. Beau gazed out the windshield into the inky black night, following the signs to the highway. "The divorce has been really hard on her," he said after a moment. "She's not exactly the person you remember. I think if she finds out that Tyler's halfway across the country, she'll lose it."

"What do you mean?" Lila asked, frowning. "Is she okay?"

Beau shook his head, his hands clenched the steering wheel. Lila thought she noticed a smudge of red on his right hand, but decided it was just the glow of the brake lights from the car in front of them. "My dad completely bailed," he said matter-of-factly. "It turns out that all that crap he used to tell me about how to be a man and a 'responsible adult' was a lie. We haven't seen him in almost two years."

"Oh, Beau, I'm so sorry . . . ," Lila whispered, stunned.

"I guess leaving my mom for some model-slash-actress-slash-whatever wasn't enough for him," Beau continued. His voice didn't sound bitter, though, just resigned. "He hasn't paid a cent in child support, and my mom doesn't have enough money to hire a lawyer."

Lila thought about the time Mr. Hodges had made her a bologna sandwich after she'd fallen off the monkey bars in Beau's backyard. He'd given her a glow-in-the-dark Band-Aid and called her scrapes battle scars. Her brain had trouble reconciling *that* Mr. Hodges with the now absentee one. She couldn't imagine how Beau pieced it all together.

"Did he move far away?" she asked.

Beau laughed, but it was a hollow sound. "He lives exactly

fifteen miles away in Sherman Oaks. It's not that he's unreach-able. He just wants to pretend he's some young guy with a hot trophy wife and a fast car. An ex-wife and two kids would kind of ruin all that."

"God," Lila said. She absently grabbed the fuzzy dice off the mirror and squeezed them hard. "That's so disgusting."

"My mom is a wreck," Beau said simply as he turned onto the ramp to the highway. "She works all the time. She's never home. She tries to hold it together for Tyler, because he's too young to know how tough things are. He can barely deal with the fact that Dad won't return his phone calls."

"He's just a kid!" Lila cringed at the familiarity of her words—it was exactly what Beau had said when she'd threatened Cooper with Santa's demise. Her cheeks flushed with shame.

"I don't care so much for me," Beau said, shrugging. "But it kills Tyler. He thinks it's his fault. Which only makes my mom worry more. So I've pretty much taken over Tyler duty. It's seri-ously the least I can do, since she doesn't want me to get a job. She thinks I should concentrate on school, be a kid, whatever." He shook his head.

Lila squeezed the dice even harder, not sure what to say.

"We have our system down," Beau said, sounding brighter. He switched lanes, passing a car going fifteen miles under the limit. "I do the whole breakfast thing, get Tyler to school, pick him up, do all that after-school stuff. She's working two jobs during the week, but still, it was working out okay—until my grandmother wiped out on her steps last week and broke her hip."

"Oh, no," Lila murmured.

"That's where my mom is right now," Beau said. He stretched his arm out along the car window and smiled slightly. "This is all a really long-winded way of telling you why I really don't want the police involved in this runaway-brothers thing either. She doesn't need one more thing to worry about."

Lila's heart panged in her chest, and her fingers itched to reach out and hug Beau, to tell him it would be okay. She imagined him getting breakfast ready in the morning for his mom and brother, packing Tyler's lunch and making sure his shoes were tied and his socks matched. No wonder he seemed so much calmer, so much more grown-up. It was what he'd told her back at his house when she'd asked when he'd turned into Mr. Maturity—he'd had no choice.

"Okay, so no police," Lila said. "For now, at least. Although our brothers may leave us no other option."

A smile twitched at the corner of Beau's mouth. "Tyler's pretty cool for a kid. And I have a sneaking suspicion that *your* little brother might grow up to be a criminal mastermind." Lila laughed at the idea. "But I refuse to believe that two eight-year-olds who still believe in Santa can consistently outwit the both of us," he said.

"Oh, yeah?" Lila said mildly, remembering the boys' impish waves from the San Jose platform.

"For one thing, we have an iPhone."

Lila laughed.

"And for another, we're actually working together now," Beau pointed out. Lila looked over at him. His eyes were blue and bright. "Which means we have a shot."

"Yeah," she agreed, smiling. "I think we do."

14

She was at her favorite Malibu beach, but it was changed, some-how, so that the water of the sparkling Pacific Ocean was as warm as the California sun overhead. She knew that if she dove in, the water would be as welcoming as a bath. But she wasn't near the water—she was leaning back against his chest, happy and safe in his arms. She could feel him behind her, his skin warm in the sunlight, and warmer still against her own.

She sighed and settled back against him. She tipped her head to the side and felt his mouth move in a beguiling line down the stretch of her neck. She didn't have to see him to *see* him—those bright blue eyes, that inky black hair, the delicious smirk he always seemed to wear—

Wait a minute—

Beau?

Lila woke up with a start.

Her heart hammered against her chest, and she looked around wildly, trying to make sense of the fact that she was in a moving car—not on a beach—though it seemed almost as bright. And much, much colder. Quickly, the events of the previous day came back to her. Cooper. Santa Claus. *Erik.* The endless road trip. Beau.

Beau, who, if she closed her eyes again, she could *feel* holding her like he had in her dream, his lips tickling her skin, sending shivers up and down her body.

She turned her head to see Beau smiling at her from behind the wheel. Same bright blue eyes. Same inky black hair. Same delicious smirk.

"Hey," he said.

"Um. Hey." She felt shy and silly. *Leftover dream confusion,* she told herself.

"Good morning," he said. He laughed. "More like good afternoon."

"Afternoon?" Lila shook her head and couldn't help a yawn. She reached to cover her mouth just in time. "Where are we?"

"The last sign I saw said we were only about twenty miles outside Seattle. We're making really good time."

"How long have I been asleep?" Lila asked, blinking. A little bit of research on Beau's iPhone back at Stanford had told them the last train to leave San Jose would take twenty hours to reach

Seattle, thanks to its various stops along the way north. But it would only take them twelve hours by car. Lila had directed Beau to Route 101, headed north, and taken the wheel just as soon as they'd gotten through San Francisco. The last thing she remembered was staggering into a bathroom in Ashland, Oregon, in a complete daze. She and Beau must have switched places again after that.

"A while," Beau said. "You missed Portland."

"Oh, bummer," Lila said. He cocked an eyebrow questioningly, and she shrugged. "I always wanted to see Portland. What was it like?"

"Cold," Beau said. "I mean, it *looked* cold. I didn't get out and personally investigate or anything."

It hit Lila then that Beau had spent untold hours next to her while she slept, and who knew how gross she was in her sleep? Did she snore? Drool? Oh, God—what if she'd drooled all over herself? Not that Beau would care. She knew he wasn't that kind of guy. Even if she *had* drooled all over herself, he'd probably just think it was funny.

She sat up and flipped down the passenger mirror. Needless to say, after an entire night and half a day cooped up in the car, she did not look her best. There were luggage compartments beneath her weary-looking brown eyes. Her SoCal-tanned skin looked pale and dry. And, oh God, her hair. She'd mastered the art of the blowout because her long, dark hair, if not properly tamed, exploded into something one could only call *wild animal*. What was staring back at her from the mirror was a *safari* of wild animal hair.

Lila attempted to minimize the damage. She smoothed her terrifying hair into something more like wild curls, and rummaged around in her bag for a little bit of lip gloss.

"Please tell me you have gum," Beau said. "My mouth tastes like the last truck stop."

"Ew," Lila said, but she found her pack of Extra Mango Smoothie gum and handed it to Beau.

"Now my mouth tastes like a *tropical* truck stop," he said a few minutes later. Lila giggled.

The drive into Seattle was pretty. The winter day was cold and sharp. Beau had jacked up the heat inside the car to compensate for their southern California clothes. She stared out the windows as they approached the city. Elliott Bay gleamed in the afternoon light, with the snowcapped Olympic Mountains rising in the distance. The Space Needle poked up like something from *The Jetsons*. The huge red cranes down on the waterfront gave way to the city, and before Lila knew it Beau was pulling up in front of the Seattle Amtrak station. The building was made of red brick and boasted a gorgeous tower that Lila thought looked out of place on a train station.

"Don't go anywhere," Beau said. He put the hazards on, and grinned at Lila. "I'll be right back."

Lila gasped at the slap of cold winter air that rushed into the car when Beau opened his door. He slammed the door behind him, but the cold remained. It was seriously winter in Seattle. Cold that even her dad would acknowledge as true winter cold. The snow on the ground was real, unlike those faux-winter scenes that Los Angelenos set up on their otherwise green and healthy lawns, beneath their palm trees. She shivered into her leather jacket, which was not going to stand up well to any real kind of chill.

A few minutes later, Beau jumped back into the car, rubbing his hands together.

He turned the heat up higher, the air rushing at them from the vents. He looked over at Lila, his blue eyes sparkling and his cheeks slightly red from the outside air. "Their train is on time—which means we have about six hours to spare."

"Six hours?" Lila laughed. "Surely you mean six seconds."

"Nope." His mouth curved into a smile. "Six hours to kill before the little monsters roll in. More than enough time to fig-ure out how to murder them."

"I thought you were on their side," Lila reminded him, raising an eyebrow. "All that stuff about how they're just little kids?"

"That was before I had to chase them up the coast into the Pacific Northwest," Beau said dryly. "It's amazing how a nine-million-hour drive will change your opinion on things."

"It really is," Lila said, and then felt shy again when their gazes met and his eyes seemed so impossibly, breathtakingly blue. Something warm bloomed inside of her and spread. She made a face to cover her embarrassment, and gestured at Seattle, spread out in front of them like a Christmas card through the windshield. "So . . . ," she said awkwardly. "What are we going to do for the next six hours?"

15

SALVATION ARMY RETAIL STORE
SEATTLE
DECEMBER 23
4:45 P.M.

"I don't know," Lila said in as serious a voice as she could manage, keeping her voice down so as not to risk any more dirty looks from the other shoppers. "I think it's really *you*."

But she couldn't keep herself from exploding into giggles at the end.

"Right?" Beau asked, grinning. He threw out his hip and tossed his arms over his head like a contestant on *Project Runway*—a show Lila was positive he had never seen. Or had he? At this point, nothing would surprise her. Beau flipped up the hood of the parka. "I'm not afraid of fashion. I embrace it."

They had decided that they were way too far north to mess around with the cold in their southern California clothes. Beau had parked the car by the Amtrak station, and they'd shivered their way to the nearest Salvation Army store—which was, happily, not too far a walk. They had then proceeded to try on winter clothes.

But only the most ridiculous winter clothes they could find. Like the down-stuffed ski overalls that Beau had first tried on. Or the flannel bodysuit that Lila had worn for a while, until the smell of mildew overpowered her. Or the bright purple and green, floor-length parka Beau was currently modeling, complete with fur-lined hood.

"I dare you," Lila said, wiping at her eyes. "I dare you to walk around in that."

Beau took another theatrical turn. The parka swung out around him like a cape. He drew the fur-lined hood up around his face like an Eskimo.

"You have no idea how warm this is," he told her. He petted the thick down-filled material, like he was seriously considering buying it.

"You look like a hooded eggplant," Lila pointed out.

Beau rolled his eyes and took off the coat.

"Fine," he pretended to sniff. "But just because you have no vision, I don't see why *I* have to suffer."

Lila snickered and turned away from him, toward a rack of winter coats. She let her fingers trail along the tops of various different monstrosities. There was an assortment of plaid, ugly bright colors, and fake fur. The coats looked like they should be worn by very old people. They probably *had* been worn by very old people.

But then she saw it. It practically *gleamed* in its awfulness— all but demanding that she stop and gawk. It was nubby and royal blue, except for the parts across the chest where it looked like a Shetland pony had died. To say nothing of the military epaulets that swung from the collar, or the leopard-print fringe that danced from the sleeves. It was half-cape, half-coat, and boasted what looked like a hanging lace train in the back. Smiling widely, she pulled it off the rack, closed her eyes as if to gather strength, and then threw it on.

"Ta-da!" she cried, jumping out from behind the rack and surprising Beau. His eyes widened and he set down the ugly plaid scarf he'd been examining.

"Oh, wow," he said. He leaned against the nearest rack and indicated she should twirl for him. Lila obliged, throwing a little pirouette in there at the end, just for fun.

"You like?" she asked, sashaying toward him like she was on a runway.

"That . . ." Beau shook his head, his eyes moving from Shetland pony to epaulets to cape. "That is the most fantastic coat I have ever seen. It completely blows the hooded eggplant away!"

Lila walked down the overstuffed aisle toward the sad, lopsided set of mirrors propped up against the far wall. She caught sight of herself in the middle one, and was nearly rendered breathless. Beau wasn't kidding—the coat was insane. And *she* looked insane wearing it.

"I think this might be the coat that ate Seattle."

"Yeah, ate it and then puked it back up, *then* made a coat out of it," Beau said.

Lila scrunched up her face. "That's revolting."

"And so is your coat," Beau said, walking up behind her. She could see him in the mirrors, and for a moment she felt almost frozen. She watched his hands come to her shoulders, and smooth their way down her arms. She realized she was holding her breath, and let it go.

The coat, she told herself, sounding breathless even in her own head. *He's just amazed by this stupid coat.*

"Who would wear something like this?" Lila asked, spreading her arms out wide, so the various hanging parts had a chance to wave.

"I think the better question is, who would design something like this in the first place?" Beau asked, laughing.

Lila shrugged, and then went still as Beau's fingers moved toward her neck. She could feel the rough edges of his fingertips against her smooth skin. She felt a heat rush through her, and it was difficult to breathe. He reached down and flipped out the collar of the coat to look for a tag. Even through the thick layers of fabric, it was like she could feel his touch all over her body.

She looked up and met Beau's gaze in the mirror. She was

aware of her heartbeat, of his closeness. His eyes bored into hers. Like they could see through her, to that secret, scared part of her she'd kept hidden away for years. She watched her own mouth fall open slightly and saw the dazed look in her eyes.

But then he stepped back, and when she turned to look at him, he was wearing that familiar old smirk of his, and his eyes were guarded.

"It has a label, Lila," he told her. "You know what that means."

"I have no idea what that means," she told him, and then busied herself with taking the hideous coat off and replacing it on its hanger.

"Lila, think." He grinned. "It means there are *more*."

They did not buy the hooded eggplant coat, or even the coat that ate Seattle—though Beau made Lila put it on again and took a few iPhone pictures of her in it, for proof.

"Proof of what?" she asked, laughing.

"Someday," Beau told her, aiming his phone at her as she posed like Victoria Beckham, one foot forward, pout on her face, "you'll think, 'Oh yeah, there was that really ugly coat in the Salvation Army.' But you'll tell yourself that it couldn't have been *that* ugly. That you're embellishing it in your memory. When that day comes"—he brandished his phone at her—"I will send you this picture."

Beau ended up with a perfectly unremarkable black coat that almost looked like he'd owned it all along. A thick knit cap and a pair of gloves, and he was ready to go. Lila chose comfort over couture and went with a dark brown quilted parka with a furry hood. She even found a pink hat and gloves that almost matched her scarf.

Outside, light snow dusted the sidewalks, though there was enough shoved to the sides to indicate a recent, heavier storm. But what Lila couldn't get over was that it was snowing *now*, flakes dancing in the air as they cascaded from the white winter sky.

"It's so pretty!" she whispered, charmed by the snowflakes that swirled around them. She caught a few of them on her tongue.

"It's a lot different from the mall," Beau said, smiling at her. Lila laughed, because he was right. Back home, she and Carly liked to take at least one trip over the hill into West Hollywood at this time of year, to experience the Christmas season at the Grove, an outdoor shopping mall. It sported Santa's house, reindeer in the sky, Christmas performances, and, every hour or so, fake snow from above. Lila had always loved it. But the real thing was so much better.

They walked along a busy shopping street, and she didn't know what pleased her more—the brightly lit shop windows, alive with bright lights and color, or the crispness of the air.

She loved the way the snowflakes stuck to her coat, and found herself giggling like a little kid as an idea came to her.

While Beau peered into the windows of an art studio, Lila scooped up some of the snow with her gloved hands and packed it together, just enough to hold.

"Hey, Beau?" She waited until he turned around, then lobbed the loose snowball directly into his face. "Merry Christmas," she said sweetly.

Beau stood stock-still for a moment and then wiped his cheeks. He met her gaze, and the look in his eyes made Lila squeal with delight and terror.

"You better run, Lila. This means war."

They dodged in and out of stores and chased each other down the street, hiding behind a parked car here or a tree there.

"Gotcha!" Beau cried, coming around a park bench way too fast and tackling Lila backward into a snowbank.

"Oomph!" Lila grunted as her back crunched into the snow. "It's not as soft as it looks," she said. She narrowed her eyes at Beau as he sprawled on top of her. "And neither are you." She lunged to the side, scooped up a handful of snow, and tried to mash it into his face.

"Yeah, right," Beau said, laughing. He swung his leg over and straddled her, easily pinning her arms down to the ground with her hands on either side of her head. Lila struggled to move her wrists out of his control, but he didn't budge. She stuck her tongue out at him. "What's your plan now?" he taunted her.

Lila gazed up at him. The city seemed to fade away around them as she got lost in his blue eyes. He leaned closer, bringing his mouth close to hers. Lila's heart stopped beating. Beau moved closer. Was this really happening? He gave her a crooked smile. Lila held her breath.

From the corner of her eye, she saw his hand come up.

Then there was ice against her face and snow in her mouth—and Beau was whooping with laughter.

"I'm going to kill you," she vowed, scrambling to her feet. Her skin was chilled through and stinging slightly. Beau laughed louder and jumped out of range. Then he took off running.

Lila ducked her head and charged after him.

"Ha!" she cried in triumph a while later, when she nailed him from her hiding place behind a tree, from a good distance. "You forget—I used to kick ass in Little League!"

"I didn't forget," Beau said, advancing on her. He picked her up and hauled her over his shoulder, pretending to hurl her into oncoming traffic. They wrestled for a moment, and Lila had to prop herself up against the side of a building once she wriggled away, in order to catch her breath. Beau leaned down to pack a snowball and winced. He looked at his knuckles, flexing them. Lila looked too. His knuckles were raw and red. A fresh cut left a streak of blood on his snowball.

"Hey," she said, frowning. "You hurt your hand!"

"I'm fine," he said.

"Except for the fact that your hand is bleeding."

Beau straightened, packing the red-streaked snowball. He looked at her as if he was considering something.

"What is it?" she asked. Suddenly she remembered the smudge on his hand back at Stanford. Had his hand been hurt all this time? "What happened?"

"I didn't just take Erik's keys from his room," Beau said, shrugging, though his eyes were steady on Lila's.

She tried to make sense of what she was hearing. "So you . . . what?" She shook her head.

"I suggested that one way he could make up for the fact he was all over some skank in front of you was to help us out," Beau said. He smirked a little bit. "It turned out he was happy to help."

"You *suggested* this," Lila said, watching Beau carefully. She glanced down at his hand. The bleeding had stopped, but there was still a cut across the knuckles and it was definitely swollen. She raised her brows. "And how exactly did you suggest it?"

Beau raised his brows right back. "I punched him."

"You punched Erik."

"Yup." Beau sounded defiant. Unashamed. "Then I kind of demanded his car keys."

Lila stared at him. He stood there challengingly, in his new black coat and hat, daring her to get mad at him. But she wasn't mad. She was . . . well, she didn't know what she was.

"Well, good," she said finally. And then she smiled. She could see her breath in big puffs in front of her. "He deserved it."

"Yeah, he did," Beau agreed. The look on his face made her mouth go dry. It was serious and sweet and protective, somehow, all at once. But she didn't have time to think about it, because he was packing a fresh snowball between his long fingers.

Lila ran.

As she laughed and dodged, she knew one thing for sure. Beau wading back into a Stanford party and punching Erik meant something. Beau wasn't exactly the angry, pick-a-fight type. He wouldn't have done that if he didn't care about her.

The only question was . . . how did she feel about him?

16

The afternoon went by in a swirl of snow and Christmas lights, and soon night fell. Lila realized that she was getting cold, despite her new winter coat. They'd been running around outside all afternoon, playing like demented puppies in the snow.

"I'm beginning to understand the appeal of seasons," Lila said as they walked down the street, weaving their way between last-minute shoppers carrying colorful packages. Even the festive shop windows, decked out in holiday splendor, looked colder now that the sun was down. She huddled a little into her coat. With the dark came a bitter wind that seemed to seep directly into her bones.

"I don't know," Beau said, his cheeks red from the last handful of snow she'd managed to smush into his face. "Snow is cool and all for, like, a day, but I like the fact that I can go surfing in January."

Lila frowned at him. "You don't surf." She tried to imagine Beau in a wet suit, jumping into the back of a jeep with Erik and his surfing buddies. The picture didn't exactly come together.

"Hell, no." Beau laughed, as if he was trying out the same image. "Have you ever talked to those dudes? I mean, not the sharpest *brahs* in the toolshed. But I *could*, if I wanted."

He drifted to a stop outside one of the many independent coffeehouses they'd passed during their epic snowball fight. This one seemed brighter than the stores around it; PERK-O-LATE, the big red sign over the coffee shop door read, with a drawing of a coffee mug with a fire lit beneath it. The big window was steamed up from the heat inside. Lila was suddenly seized by the desire for a piping hot mocha latte, with extra whipped cream.

"Check it out," Beau said, pointing at a hand-lettered sign in the front window. "Open mic night."

"You left your guitar in the car," Lila protested.

Beau only smiled and pushed open the door, waving Lila indoors in front of him.

She paused the moment she crossed the threshold, soaking in the rush of coffee-scented heat and background music. The walls were painted bright gold and blue, and every spare inch was covered with movie posters. Booths were built along the far wall, and the rest of the space was filled with comfy armchairs, upholstered stools, and square dark wood tables. Seattleites lounged at the tables, black sweaters and ripped jeans mixed with hippie dresses and dyed-white punk rock hair.

"Grab us a table, and I'll get you a drink," Beau said.

Lila accepted his offer with a nod. She thought back to last night in Big Sur, when she'd been starving but hadn't wanted Beau to buy her so much as a gas station snack. God, had she really turned down *food*? What was she thinking?

She wove her way through the tables, and found a little booth toward the back. She flopped down, happy to peel off her heavy outer layers and relax in the warm atmosphere of the coffee shop. It was a cool spot. Coffee shops in L.A. were filled with jerks with laptops, trying to be "screenwriters" while hogging the best tables all day long. But Perk-O-Late seemed to veer toward the hipster crowd without actually wallowing in that scene. For every pair of skinny jeans with a facial piercing, there was someone in a North Face jacket and Timberlands. They all looked like cool people who might spontaneously go on a hike. There was a small stage set up in front of the big window overlooking the street, and on it stood a hippie-chic girl, singing some kind of folk/punk hybrid. Her blue-tinted hair swayed slightly as she played her guitar.

Beau is much better, Lila noted.

She jumped a little bit in her seat when Beau appeared before her as if summoned, setting down two heavy mugs piled high with whipped cream. Lila felt herself blushing, like she'd been picturing him naked or something.

Which she then proceeded to do—and *really* felt her cheeks burst into flames.

He eased into the booth. "What's going on in there?" he asked mildly, his eyes laughing. Like he already knew.

Lila reached for the mug closest to her. "Yum," she said, embarrassed to hear the huskiness in her own voice. "A mocha latte with almost more whipped cream than coffee, I hope." Suddenly it occurred to her that he hadn't asked her what she wanted. She faltered, her gaze rising to his.

He'd known. He'd remembered.

"Almost," Beau said. A smile played around his mouth. "There's some caffeine in there, too. We still have miles to go before we sleep."

"I love that poem," Lila said in a whisper.

Beau leaned back in his seat. "I know."

She had to look away from him then, because her eyes felt too hot and his saw too much. So she picked up a spoon and dug out a serious chunk of the whipped cream. It was the good stuff—homemade and thick and sweet. She licked up a mouthful like it was ice cream.

"This might be the best thing I've ever tasted," she said in a normal voice, breaking the spell between them.

Beau drank a little bit from his own mug, but he was practically humming with nervous energy. He unzipped his coat and shrugged out of his hoodie. It felt like déjà vu to see his ratty concert T-shirt again. Beau standing in his basement, glaring at her, felt like it had happened in a different lifetime.

"Want to get up there?" he asked, nodding toward the stage as the folk/punk girl concluded her set and everyone around them applauded.

"Up where?" Lila asked, pretending not to understand.

"Come on." He grinned at her. "We're in a different state, so I don't think it counts if you perform with me here. It won't affect your whole *the state of California will fall into the ocean before I sing with you again* mandate."

"Oh, yeah," Lila said, embarrassed. She stuck her finger into her whipped cream and pulled out a big dollop. "I did say that, didn't I?" She couldn't believe he remembered it, word for word. She licked away the whipped cream, full of cinnamon and sugar and the hint of mocha below.

"Yelled it, actually. More than once." But he was smiling.

Lila shrugged and blew on her coffee. The liquid was still burning hot. And so were her cheeks.

"Impressive memory," she said, deciding not to bring up what *he* had said: that if she wanted to hang out with zombies like Carly Hollander, she could go right ahead and do that. And not to worry about singing with him, because he'd rather never sing again than sing with her.

"Well," Beau said quietly. "Any chance you'll reconsider?"

Lila shook her head, looking away from him.

"You go," she said. "If you want. I'm a really good audience member."

He shrugged, and she had to blink a few times at her mocha to clear the sudden fog in her eyes. When she looked up, Beau had somehow talked the previous folk/punk girl out of her guitar and was settling onto the stage like he owned it.

Lila sat back in her chair and prepared to lead the cheering section.

"Hi," Beau said. "I'm visiting from California. Thought I'd play a few songs." He strummed a chord, then smiled that killer, crowd-pleasing smile of his. "Oh, yeah," he said. "I'm Beau."

A table of girls near the front burst into applause. Lila shook her head. She should have known he wouldn't need any help winning over the entire coffee shop. Beau lived and breathed the stage. And he could read a crowd better than anyone she'd ever met. Which was no doubt why he took one look at the hipster-but-not-too-hip clientele and began to play an acoustic, mellow version of Gwen Stefani's "Hollaback Girl." The crowd loved it.

"I ain't no hollaback girl," Beau sang, in his scratchy, soulful voice. Three guys in skinny jeans leapt up and started cheering. Then they sang along.

Lila looked on in disbelief. So Beau *did* listen to pop music! Enough to cover a Gwen Stefani song, anyway.

She didn't know if she wanted to hit him or hug him. Maybe both.

"You guys are great," Beau said after a few songs. He scraped his thick dark hair back from his face, calling attention to how impossibly blue his eyes were. "But I feel like something's missing." He trailed off and searched the crowd. "I need a front woman."

"Me!" cried one of the girls in front, throwing her hands in the air. She jumped up and down in her combat boots, her goth black hair flying around her face, her purple tights gleaming.

"I would," Beau said with his flirtiest grin, "but I have a good feeling about that girl right back there."

He pointed at Lila. The entire crowd swiveled around to stare at her. She froze mid-sip. Great. She probably had whipped cream on her nose.

"Her name is Lila," Beau told the coffee house. "And she has a song she wants to sing for you, but she's shy."

"Don't be shy! Be a warrior woman!" cried the folk/punk chick with blue-tinted hair.

Lila wanted to die. Actually, she wanted to kill Beau, and *then* die.

"*Li*-la! *Li*-la! *Li*-la!" the crowd chanted.

What else could she do but get up and join him on the makeshift stage?

"You're a dead man," she told Beau when she got there, furious and embarrassed all at once. Staring out at all the eager, waiting faces, she felt her heart start beating double-time. "I hate you," she added.

"That's code for 'I love you,'" Beau told the audience.

"Whoo-hooooo!" they cheered.

Before Lila could respond, he started playing the opening chords of that old song of theirs, the one that he'd sung in Big Sur. And just as she had then, Lila felt herself drawn back in time, back into the safe cocoon of those Friday nights they'd spent with their guitars, sprawled across Beau's bed.

Those days were gone, but when she caught Beau's eye, none of that seemed to matter. He smiled at her. And she sang.

The words came back to her with ease, but what shocked her, after years of never doing more than singing in the shower, was how easy it was to slip back into singing, even in front of a crowd.

And how easy it was to sing with Beau.

"Let me just say that gifts are cool, though allergies make me feel a fool," they sang together. *"Roses are red and violets are blue, and animals are better off in the zoo."*

They easily picked up their familiar harmony, and Lila had to admit that she loved it. She'd missed the joy of it all, the way her voice and the guitar and Beau's voice all melded together and sounded so perfect, so effortless. She couldn't believe she'd forgotten how much she'd loved it. She felt happy and free straight down to her toes.

"Maybe this spring fever will pass, maybe I'm acting like an ass," they sang to each other and to the audience. *"Maybe the flu will do us in, and maybe your heart's not mine to win."*

And when the song was done, everyone in the coffee house jumped to their feet. Lila laughed in delight and turned toward Beau.

But whatever words she'd been about to say died on her tongue the second she saw his eyes. They were deep and blue and saw her—all of her—from her fuzzy seventh-grade hair to their perfect harmony, and everything in between. The air around them seemed thick and the audience faded into nothing. All Lila could think was how much she wanted him to kiss her.

And then he did.

His mouth felt so familiar—and so different. Warm and sweet and with an underlying kick that made her whole body shake. She kissed him back, heedless and happy, one hand curling into his thick hair.

The audience went wild.

"Encore!" they shouted.

Encore, indeed.

17

Lila could feel the cold slap of the winter wind the moment they stepped back outside, leaving the warmth of the coffee house behind them. The difference was, she didn't care anymore. She felt warmed from the inside out. She couldn't seem to look away from Beau, and neither of them could stop smiling. It was like they were lighting up the Seattle dusk with their smiles. Beau kissed her again, right there on the sidewalk.

He took his time, lingering against her lips and holding her face between his hands. When he pulled back slightly, he smiled even wider and then kissed her again.

"I just want to make sure that wasn't, you know, a trick of the stage lights," Beau murmured against her mouth.

"There weren't any stage lights, you idiot," Lila replied affectionately, standing on her tiptoes and kissing him as the snow swirled around them. She felt like she was in one of those shake-up snow globes that her mother collected. Like there was a bubble around the two of them, and maybe the city of Seattle had been arranged around them just to enhance the perfect, Christmassy moment.

Beau pulled away and slung an arm over Lila's shoulders. It was like a puzzle piece clicking into place. It was crazy how well they fit together—and Lila remembered, suddenly, how well they always had.

"Seems real," Beau drawled. "But I might have to check again. . . ."

She stuck her tongue out at him and then glanced at her watch. Her stomach dropped to the ground with a sickening lurch, and she stopped dead.

"What?" Beau asked, his hand lingering on her neck.

"Oh my God," Lila managed to say. She waved her wrist at Beau like a crazy person. He only stared back at her, not comprehending. "The *train*!" she practically screamed in panic. "It's arriving in ten minutes!"

Beau swore, loudly and rudely enough to attract the offended stares of two nearby ladies in fake Uggs. But then they were running again—slipping and sliding down the wintry Seattle sidewalks, weaving in and out of the crowds of pedestrians getting in their last-minute Christmas shopping.

"How could we let this happen?" Lila shrieked.

Beau didn't respond until they came to a skidding halt at a traffic light. He bounced up and down on his feet, impatient.

"We can't let them get past us here," he said in a low voice. "If they find a way to sneak across the border . . ."

Lila's hands were in fists at her sides, her breath coming in giant puffs in the frozen air.

"They'll be in Canada," she finished flatly. "And we don't have passports."

"Exactly," Beau said. "We're screwed."

The traffic light changed.

"Better run," Lila said.

So they did.

Lila was out of breath, and even Beau was breathing hard by the time they reached the Amtrak station. Beau threw open the doors, and Lila collided with his back as he came to a halt. Beau muttered something and used his arm to usher Lila around the pile of suitcases he'd almost tripped over. It seemed like the entire city of Seattle was milling around in the train station. It was almost Christmas Eve Day, after all. Lila skirted the edge of the porter's trolley, nearly bruising her shins, only to narrowly avoid being knocked down by a couple who refused to separate their clasped hands. They wove their way through the crowd of people, fighting to get in front of the big arrivals board.

Lila glimpsed the track number, next to the bright digital time: 9:37. "This way!" she shouted, taking off. There was no time to think about the fact that, according to the board, the train was *arriving*. Did that mean in a few minutes, or did that mean right now? Lila pumped her arms and legs and tried to make her tired body move faster than it ever had before. Beau sprinted ahead of her, vaulting over another pile of luggage.

Lila got her answer moments later as she followed Beau to the right track. They skidded to a stop at the end of the platform and saw that the train was still moving, pulling into the station at this very second. The moonlight gleamed on its shiny silver exterior.

"Thank God." Lila's whole body sighed with relief.

Beau yanked his hat down over his ears. "We don't have them yet."

The good news was that the train ended its run in Seattle, so everybody had to disembark. There would be no games this time, the way there had been in San Jose. The boys would have to transfer trains in order to go north into Canada. Which, Lila knew, didn't mean there wouldn't be *other* games. She'd be an idiot to underestimate Cooper now.

Lila and Beau moved down the platform as the train's doors opened and the passengers began to pour out. They traveled in packs, lugging suitcases behind them, bottlenecking at the train doors. There were so many people exiting from so many doors, it was hard to imagine being able to pick out just two.

"Great," Beau muttered.

"Just look for the short people." Lila scanned the crowd for Cooper's brown cowlicked head.

Her heart sank. The platform was a zoo. There were so many people—the passengers from the train and the people meeting them. Whole families arriving and searching for their loved ones—because, duh, it was Christmas.

Beau dove to the left and came within inches of attempting to kidnap a little kid who was definitely *not* his brother.

"Sorry," he murmured as the little boy's mother glared at him and hustled her child away.

"Oops," he whispered to Lila. She winced in sympathy but couldn't muster the energy to tease him.

"Did we miss them?" She scanned the now-thinning lines of passengers exiting the train doors. Were they hiding somewhere onboard? Could they have done something *really* crazy, like jump off the train before it hit the station? Lila's stomach twisted as she treated herself to an image of Cooper leaping from a moving train, hitting the frozen ground . . .

No, she told herself. *We will find him. That's it. Nothing else is possible.*

There were so many people, and way too many kids. No one seemed to notice that they were jostling and shoving Lila.

She tried to ignore the screaming reunions, the impromptu Christmas carols, the noise, and the crush. Too many bulky coats and shopping bags. Too much noise—louder than any football rally Lila had ever attended. Someone rolled a suitcase over her foot, and she barely spared a moment to see if it hurt.

Lila's panic spread through her stomach and took up residence as a lump in her throat. The boys could be right in front of her and she wouldn't necessarily see them.

Her eyes snagged, suddenly, on a patch of green in the crowd.

She grabbed Beau's arm. "Beau. Look. By the bench."

He looked. Lila couldn't move for a long moment, too busy taking in the sight of Cooper. His eyes were wide and worried, and he looked a little worse for wear—though he'd probably gotten a much better night's sleep than Lila had. He and Tyler huddled together by the bench. Cooper was holding on to his backpack like it was a teddy bear, chewing on his lower lip nervously.

Good, Lila thought, her eyes narrowing. *He* should *be nervous.*

"Come on," Beau said, his voice gravelly and commanding. He sounded like a grown-up. A pissed-off grown-up, who had absolutely no doubts about the outcome of this scenario.

Lila wasn't so sure. What if Cooper bolted? What if he claimed Lila and Beau were abducting him? She wouldn't put anything past him at this point.

Lila followed Beau as he cut through the crowd, looping around behind the bench where their brothers sat together, looking smaller and more pathetic the more they stood there, almost swallowed up by the chaos of the holiday crowd. Obviously worried that the boys might run, Beau indicated with hand gestures that Lila should go around one end of the bench while he took the other. Keeping their eyes on each other, they circled the boys, until they had them cornered.

"Oh," Cooper said when he saw them.

"Oh?" Lila echoed, all the tension and panic leaking out of her body. "That's all you have to say?"

But she wasn't as mad as she expected to be. In fact, looking at his freckles and his little face with a chocolate smudge on one cheek and his hair standing on end, she had the completely unexpected urge to hug him. It was almost as strong as her urge to choke him with her bare hands. He was maddening, but he was her brother, and she couldn't deny that she was glad to find him all in one piece.

Not that she planned to tell him that.

"I have to rescue Santa!" Cooper cried, his eyes wide and serious. "It's an emergency!"

"Santa can take care of himself," Beau interjected, flicking a look at Lila. He had one hand on Tyler's shoulder, and Lila couldn't tell if he was doing some kind of guy almost-hug thing, or if he was making sure his brother didn't take off. Again.

"But—"

"He's been around how long now?" Lila asked, following Beau's lead as he started to walk through the crowd, propelling Tyler before him. Cooper let his sneakers scuff against the concrete floor a little more than was necessary, but he followed too. Lila stayed just slightly behind him—prepared to tackle him to the ground if he so much as *thought* about running for it.

"The ice caps!" Tyler cried. "What about the ice caps!"

Beau threw an exasperated look at Lila over his shoulder. His meaning was clear: *This is your mess. Clean it up.*

She rolled her eyes but nodded.

"Guys," she said, as they stepped out onto the street in front of the station. The cold Seattle twilight surrounded them. "Are we talking about Santa Claus here, or what?"

"So?" Cooper demanded.

"Does he or does he not possess *flying reindeer*?" Lila asked in her best *are you dumber than Paris Hilton?* voice. "And does he or does he not have an entire workshop of elves?"

Tyler looked hopeful behind his rapidly fogging Harry Potter glasses. But Cooper just scowled.

"So what?" Cooper asked. "What does that have to do with global warming?"

"I think Santa can handle himself," Lila said with a sniff. "He manages to make Christmas happen every year. He flies around the world and delivers presents to billions of houses. Plus he knows who's been naughty or nice. What's a little warm weather compared to that?"

They arrived at Erik's car. Cooper and Tyler stared at it in confusion.

"My sister's boyfriend's car," Cooper said after a moment, rolling his eyes at Tyler, like that was a punch line. Tyler sighed in commiseration.

Lila wondered if Beau bristled at the word *boyfriend*, but she didn't dare look.

"Just get in," she ordered them.

Beau turned to look at her as they ushered the boys into the backseat, his mouth quirking up in the corner like he was fighting a smile.

"I love that snotty voice of yours," he told her. "Especially when you use it for good instead of evil."

Lila wanted to climb into his arms again, but Cooper and Tyler were in the backseat. More importantly, they had entire states—and about eighteen hours—to drive through if they wanted to beat her parents home by tomorrow night. So she only smiled and climbed into the passenger seat. Then, remembering Cooper's escapades, she clicked the child safety lock.

"You didn't have to do that," Cooper said sulkily.

"You're lucky you're not bound and gagged in the trunk," Lila told him without turning around. Beau started the car.

"Fine," Cooper said. "But I want McDonald's."

5 KATE BRIAN

"Well, I want you in the trunk," Lila said, craning her head around to glare at him as Beau pulled out into traffic and started the long drive toward home.

Cooper's mouth twitched, like he couldn't decide whether to laugh or pout.

"If you *don't* put me in the trunk," he said, "I'll give you your phone back."

Lila realized as soon as he said it that she'd completely forgotten about it. How weird was that? When her dad had so often threatened to surgically remove it from her ear?

Everything that she'd forgotten about while she'd been so caught up with Beau rushed back to her then: her party that had been hijacked and no doubt thrown beautifully—if traitorously—by Yoon. Erik's betrayal. Her entire life at North Valley High, that she'd stopped thinking about somewhere around Oregon the night before. Even now, remembering everything that had seemed so critical to her, she felt an odd distance from it all.

She wasn't sure if she wanted the phone back. It was like she was afraid to reconnect with it, with who she was when she had it.

But that was crazy. She could handle a cell phone. She stared her brother down, extended her hand, and waited.

"Fine." Cooper sighed dramatically and slapped the phone into her hand. "But if you put me in the trunk, I'm telling."

"Go ahead," Lila suggested. "Tell. Be sure to explain how you happened to be in Seattle in the first place."

"You'll get in trouble!" Cooper warned her.

"Sure," Lila said. Her eyebrows rose. "But so will you."

When she faced forward again, Beau was grinning.

"What?" she whispered.

"I told you," he said. He looked at her quickly, then back at the snow-covered road. "It's that voice."

Lila settled back in her seat and tried to get comfortable for the long drive ahead of them. She fiddled with her phone for a moment but waited until Beau was pulling onto the freeway to check her messages. She blinked as she stared at the screen. There had to be like a million texts and who knew how many voice mails. All of them from Erik.

She opened the first text, after checking to make sure Beau was still scowling at the road. It was dated the night before, right about the time Beau had picked her up in Erik's car.

I SUCK. SO SORRY. CAN'T APOLOGIZE ENOUGH. PLS CALL. I LOVE YOU.

Lila gulped in a quick breath. She looked at Beau again. Their song played in her head, and she felt that warmth inside, spreading out from within. She could still feel his kisses on her mouth, his hands against her skin. She could still see the way he looked at her, like he really, truly saw her.

She scrolled through the menu and with one last peek at Beau's bruised knuckles, selected DELETE ALL.

18

As Lila pulled off the 405 South onto the 118 for the final freeway push toward their hometown, she felt a flush of victory. Sure, it was Sunday evening and Christmas Eve, night had fallen again, and she thought her poor butt might never stop aching from all the sitting around. But she was nearly home. She had somehow, some way, rescued this weekend from the jaws of total defeat. Her body thrummed along with the car. Anxiety and triumph mixed in her belly.

Or maybe that was the Chicken McNuggets.

It also didn't hurt that Beau was sprawled out in the seat next to her, his fine body so close to hers. He never really touched her with their brothers so nearby, though every now and then their little fingers would brush against each other over the console. His arctic blue eyes warmed whenever they connected with hers.

He was slouched down low at the moment, looking a little dazed as he stared out at the road in front of them. He rubbed at his face, where the beginnings of a five o'clock shadow had taken hold. Lila shivered. It was weird to think of Beau as a *man* in that way.

Down in the little bucket between the seats, Lila's phone began to rattle against the plastic sides and Erik's CDs, vibrating loudly. Ignoring the no-handset law, she snatched it up.

"Lila?"

Of course, it was her mother.

"Hi, Mom!" Lila singsonged, widening her eyes at Beau to communicate the gravity of this call. Her whole body tensed up.

"Merry Christmas Eve!" her mother cried. Lila laughed a little bit—her mom could be such a dork.

"Yeah, Mom," she said. "You too." It suddenly occurred to Lila that her mother's insistence on preserving Cooper's belief in Santa might be about more than keeping Cooper innocent. Her mom loved the holiday. Maybe she just wanted a fantasy to hold on to too.

"How's the weekend going?" her mother asked. "I seem to have missed you several times already. Cooper said you made delicious cookies."

Lila glanced at her crafty little brother in the rearview mirror. *Cookies*? He'd invented *cookies*?

"It's been fine," Lila said. "You know. Cookies are always good." She heard Cooper giggle in the backseat, the little liar. She focused on the phone call.

"I trust everything there is as it should be," her mother said. Lila could envision her mother's arched eyebrow and crossed arms, like she was *looking* for something to be angry about. Lila was tempted to launch into some speech about how great it was to spend this time with Cooper, but sanity intervened. Her mother would never believe her if she oversold it like that. Especially not with the way things had been left between them.

"Everything's fine, Mom," Lila said in a slightly huffy tone, the one that she usually used when annoyed by her parents. The tone felt oddly put-on, like it fit as poorly as the Coat That Ate Seattle.

"Yes, well, your father and I are making much better time than we expected," Mrs. Beckwith continued. "We're running a couple of hours early, so we should see you soon."

"Soon?" Lila echoed, panic cramping her stomach. "Um, great!"

"Let me say a quick hello to your brother," Lila's mom continued. Lila handed the phone to Cooper in the backseat. Immediately she slammed her foot down on the gas. She had to get home, now.

"Lila . . ." Beau said, finally sitting up. "You're going a little fast, don't you think?" Lila flicked her gaze over at him, then back at the road. This from the person who had practically off-roaded in the Escort, requiring that whole mechanic pit stop in Big Sur.

"My parents are almost home!" she said fiercely, scowling at the road as she wove in and out of traffic. Why did people have to drive so slowly? It was *Christmas Eve*. Didn't they have places to go? "I did not go through all of this to get busted *now*, a half hour from home!"

"I get that," Beau said. "Really, I do. But you need to slow down."

"I'll slow down when my parents walk in the door to find me and Cooper calmly relaxing, with no sign of any party or anything else," Lila retorted. "Maybe even playing a friendly game of Parcheesi. With Christmas cookies on the table."

"What's Parcheesi?" Cooper asked from the backseat.

"It's a boring board game," Tyler told him.

Beau sighed. "Lila—"

All of a sudden the blare of an alarm sounded. Lila looked in the rearview mirror and saw flashing red and blue lights.

"Oh, crap." She slammed the back of her head against the headrest and groaned. She reminded herself to breathe, and guided the car over to the shoulder of the freeway. Next to her, Beau was sitting up straight, raking his hands through his hair with a grim look around his mouth.

"I can't believe this," Lila hissed. She looked at her watch. Six

ten. Her mother had said *soon*. How soon was *soon*? "We don't
have time for this—and you know they never just give you the
ticket. They always make you wait for it, too."

"I don't think a speeding ticket is really the biggest concern
here," Beau said in a low, not very friendly voice.

Lila shot him a glare, wondering what his problem was, but
she didn't have the chance to ask. The police officer had made
it to the driver's side window and was gesturing for her to roll
it down.

Lila wished that she hadn't been trapped in a stale-smelling
car with three guys for twenty hours. She wished that she had
showered sometime in recent memory. She wished that her hair
was not piled on the top of her head haphazardly, and that she'd
had the foresight to apply some lip gloss and mascara at the last
rest stop. But none of her wishes were going to help her out, so
she just smiled widely at the officer.

"License and registration, please," he said, in that measured
tone cops always used. Lila swallowed and rifled through her
bag for her license as Beau did the same with the glove compartment, looking for Erik's registration.

Which was when the reality of the situation hit her.

Lila handed over her license and the paperwork, trying to
keep herself composed until the officer walked back toward his
car.

"Oh my God," she whispered, panicking but keeping her

voice low. "Oh, *crap!*" She reached over and grabbed Beau's wrist. His skin was warm beneath her palm. "What if Erik reported his car stolen? We're going to get arrested." Her voice was more a squeak than any other sound.

"Arrested?" Tyler asked from the backseat in a hushed tone.

"Cool!" Cooper whooped. "Will we get fingerprinted?"

Beau looked less enthused at the prospect.

"Considering I punched him out to get his car keys, he probably *did* report it stolen," Beau said in a tight voice. "Which is why I told you to slow down."

"Forgive me for not taking into account all the possible outcomes of your decision to jack my boyfriend's car," Lila said sarcastically, letting her panic get the better of her. How could she have been so stupid? When she had been *this close* to making it through this weekend free and clear? "My bad."

"What's the matter with you?" he asked, frowning at Lila.

"Me?" she retorted, dropping his arm like it had burned her. "Maybe *you* shouldn't have stolen the car, or punched out my boyfriend, for that matter!"

Beau snorted. His mouth twisted, and something moved through his eyes. "Or maybe you shouldn't have had such a jerk for a *boyfriend*." His voice rested on the word for a second, a flicker passing over his eyes. Just as quickly as it came, it was gone. "What did you expect?"

And suddenly, it was like they were sucked back in time,

across three years, back into the middle of that nasty post-breakup conversation outside the cafeteria, right after Beau had found out what Lila had done with her weekend. *Erik Hollander?* Beau had asked her, sneering, like he was saying *Adolf Hitler.* He'd stared at her like he hated her, like the fact she'd gotten together with Erik on Saturday when she'd broken up with him on Friday made her the worst person in the world.

Except this time, Lila didn't care if she hurt Beau's feelings. This time, a part of her *wanted* to hurt him—wanted to make him feel, once and for all, how trapped she'd felt with him, how he'd abandoned her to nurse his fury and pain about his parents and she hadn't known what else to do but escape.

"And why do you think I did that?" she asked coldly. Meanly. She shifted around in her seat so she could look right at him—and get the full view of his shaggy hair and *screw you* posture. How had she overlooked it? So what if underneath all that he was hot? He was still Beau. He might have changed, but he was still the same person. "Why do you think Erik was so appealing after all those years with you?"

"Funny," Beau snapped back. "That's a question I've actually spent some time considering, Lila. And I always come back to the same answer. Are you sure you want to hear it?"

"You obviously want me to hear it," Lila said acidly, fighting off the déjà vu. They had had this conversation, hadn't they?

Beau turned to look at her with a gleam in his eyes that sent something cold through Lila's gut.

"You're vain and selfish," Beau said. Matter-of-factly. Like it was the simple, unvarnished truth, known to everyone in Los Angeles. "Or at least, you *choose* to be. It was probably a relief to be with someone who only required that you worship him, and never bothered you about being, I don't know, a real person. And now look at you." His eyes were hard. "You're so dedicated to being superficial that you had to be reminded how to sing— the one thing you used to really love."

Lila's mouth actually fell open in shock. Had he really just said that? In that calm, nasty way—that *rehearsed* way? Like he'd been practicing saying it to her for three years? God, he'd probably even written a song about it.

"That might hurt," she threw at him, "if it came from someone a little bit less self-righteous."

"That's hilarious—," he began.

"You get off on thinking the worst about people," she snapped. "Do you really think that every single other classmate of ours in North Valley High is a mindless zombie, yet somehow you, Beau Hodges, have seen the light? Does believing that make you feel special? Let you think you're better than everyone else? Because guess what, Beau: You're not. You're not special. You're no one."

There was a brief, charged silence as they glared at each

other. Lila felt her heart hammering against the walls of her chest. Cars zoomed past them on the freeway, rocking the Maxima slightly. In the backseat, Cooper and Tyler sat stock-still, eyes wide, drinking in this fight like it was another chocolate milk shake. If Lila hadn't been so furious, she might have been embarrassed.

"I might be *no one*," Beau said snidely. "But at least I'm not *someone* who endangered my brother's life by not calling the police—all because I want a stupid car."

Lila opened her mouth to fight away the accusation that hung in the air between them like some kind of poison gas—but movement at her window caught her attention.

"Here you go," the officer said gravely, handing Lila her documents. She braced herself. Would he handcuff her? What if he handcuffed *Cooper*?

"Thank you, officer," she murmured politely, trying to look sweet, and not like someone who would be accused of being shallow and self-centered and life-endangering by a guy she'd been kissing some twenty hours before—not to mention once or twice while the boys were sleeping during the long drive south.

"I understand that it's Christmas Eve and those boys need to get ready for Santa," the policeman said, nodding toward the backseat, where the two little boys sat up straight. The officer looked back at Lila. "I'm going to let you go with a warning. But slow down, miss."

"Thank you," Lila breathed.

But the jubilation that should have accompanied escaping the ticket—not to mention jail time for grand theft auto—failed to materialize.

Lila started up the car and pulled back into traffic. They were twenty minutes from home. A quick glance at her watch told her it was 6:28 p.m. Beau stared straight ahead, his jaw tight and his arms crossed. Lila swallowed and glared fiercely at the road. Even Cooper and Tyler were quiet.

They had beaten all the odds, a train, two devious eight-year-olds, and the California Highway Patrol. But the horrible things that she and Beau had said to each other just hung there, ruining everything.

There was no taking them back.

19

BECKWITH HOUSE
LOS ANGELES
DECEMBER 24
6:48 P.M.

Lila took the corner on to her street much faster than she should have, but Beau didn't even flinch. He just stared straight ahead, stone-faced and silent. He seemed as remote and forbidding as the Santa Monica Mountains that rose up in the distance.

Terrific, Lila thought. *At least this day can't possibly get any worse.*

She pulled into her driveway and braked in horror as her stomach dropped. She clenched her hands on the steering wheel and stared straight ahead, frozen into place.

Her parents' gray Prius sat in front of the garage, waiting for them. A quick glance at the house confirmed that all the lights were blazing. Mr. and Mrs. Beckwith were definitely home.

This day had just gotten a whole lot worse.

Tears pricked the back of Lila's eyes. How could she have

come so close to pulling this whole thing off, only to lose it all at the last second?

"Mom and Dad are home!" Cooper cried from the backseat. "Yay!"

"Hooray," Lila said sourly.

"Do you want to stay and help us decorate our tree?" Cooper asked Tyler in that same excited voice. "We always do it on Christmas Eve."

Lila squeezed her eyes closed for a moment, then opened them again. Her parents' car was still there, taunting her from its position directly in front of the garage. She waited for Beau to say something—to make her feel worse about it as only he could. But he just unlocked the backseat and herded the boys out into the evening air. He took the winter coat he'd bought at the Salvation Army store in Seattle and tossed it into the backseat, as if discarding the memories of their time there without a backward glance. Swallowing, Lila did the same.

Outside, the evening air was fragrant with night-blooming jasmine, and the sound of wind chimes and far-off traffic. It was noticeably warmer than it had been in snowy Seattle. Still, Lila shivered and crossed her arms over herself, as though they might protect her from her parents' wrath.

"I have to go to the bathroom," Tyler said, frowning up at Beau.

"Okay," Beau said. He deigned to look at Lila then, his eyebrows high, a deep chill in his blue eyes.

"Sure," Lila said, hating that look but not knowing what to do about it. Especially with her life about to end. "Come on in."

Maybe with Beau and Tyler there, her parents' fury would have to be put on hold for a while. She didn't even feel that bad about putting Beau in the middle of it, after all the things he'd just said to her.

What about what you said to him? asked a traitorous voice inside her. Lila ignored it and followed Cooper up to the house.

It was funny how the front hall looked exactly the same as when Lila had left it, even though Lila herself felt so different. The same dark hardwood floors, with the green and white area rug in the center. The same mirror over the same black chest against the wall. She pulled the door closed behind their ragged little party and told herself to breathe. There were voices coming from the family room. *They are going to kill me. I may never leave this house again.*

Cooper took off at top speed toward the family room, with Tyler close behind. Lila walked toward her own demise a little more slowly, pretending she was completely unaware of and unmoved by Beau's silent, disapproving presence behind her.

She was so focused on *not* paying attention to Beau and *not* reacting to Beau and *not* appearing to even remember that Beau existed that she found herself standing in the family room in front of her parents, blinking in confusion when she saw that they were standing there with . . .

"Erik?"

But she didn't see him standing in front of her—she saw him back at that party at Stanford, his hands all over that other girl, his mouth practically inhaling her. Lila had no idea what he was doing in her house.

It couldn't possibly be good.

She was only dimly aware that Erik was talking to her parents. Her ears were ringing, and her heart was pounding erratically in her chest. Her vision dimmed. Erik had told her parents what happened, obviously. That she had been cavorting all over the West Coast in a car Beau had stolen from him—after *assaulting* him. That she had lost Cooper for thirty hours.

How on earth would she ever explain all of that away?

Lila looked up as her mother stepped toward her, her face smooth and her eyes bright. She gave her daughter a kiss on the cheek, then smiled.

What?

"Hello, Beau," Mrs. Beckwith said. Was that *warmth* Lila heard in her mother's voice?

"Hi, Mrs. Beckwith," Beau said at once, scrupulously polite. He nodded at Lila's father. "Sir. Merry Christmas."

"Merry Christmas!" Lila's mother said happily, while Mr.

Beckwith only nodded in return from his spot on the couch. He stretched out his legs on the ottoman and linked his hands behind his head, giving everyone a perfect view of his *No, I Will Not Fix Your Computer* T-shirt, which he always claimed was a big hit with his computer geek buddies at work. He looked relaxed—*not* on the verge of grounding his daughter for life. Mrs. Beckwith smiled again, even wider, completely freaking Lila out. "Did you have fun at the planetarium?"

Lila's gaze shot to Erik. As if he had been waiting for her to give him some sign, he strolled over and wrapped his arm around her shoulders like he had never cheated on her—like he expected her to snuggle up against him. He seemed so much bigger than she remembered. His arm was bulky and heavy, and he had to angle himself down to kiss her on the cheek. Lila wanted to shake him off and wipe her cheek, but she didn't understand what was going on. What game was Erik playing? He didn't seem to notice how stiffly she held herself—or the intense look Beau threw at him. But Lila did, and she registered every second of it.

"I told your parents that I was holding down the fort around here while you guys took the rug rats to look at some stars," Erik told her. His voice sounded too hearty. Fake. Lila stared at him. He was no longer the Erik she remembered—that glowing, gorgeous creature who effortlessly compelled everyone in the room to adore him. Instead, all she saw was frat guy Erik, who wasn't as cute as he thought he was, and who had put on the freshman fifteen. Probably in beer. Or skanks.

Not to mention the shiner he was sporting on his left eye.

Erik reached over and patted Cooper on the back, like he and Cooper were such great buddies, when Lila was fairly certain Erik had never once spoken to Cooper in the three years they'd dated. But he patted too hard, and Cooper went stumbling forward a few feet. Beau reached out and steadied him, shooting Erik another unfriendly look.

But neither of Lila's parents seemed to notice.

They were too busy watching Erik smile at Lila. They loved him, Lila thought in dawning understanding, because he seemed so safe and dependable. He was always well mannered. He wasn't unpredictable or moody or artistic, like Beau.

"Did you have fun?" Erik asked, smiling wider, squeezing her slightly in warning. Her parents smiled too, waiting for Lila to talk about the fictional planetarium trip that Erik had obviously made up. To confirm that it had happened. The two boys looked at her, waiting to see what she would say. She could feel Beau's gaze too, and she couldn't imagine what he thought of all this.

But then, suddenly, Lila got it. This was her get-out-of-jail-free card. Erik was covering for her. This was his way out of saying he wanted her back. All she had to do was play along and she would get that car on her birthday and be free for the rest of her senior year.

Free. She wouldn't have to depend on anyone else to get around, to go where she wanted to go. She wouldn't have permanently lost her parents trust and respect. *Completely free at last.*

"You guys caught the light show, isn't that right, babe?" Erik prodded. It was a perfect, brilliant lie. Her parents would be delighted that Lila had actually taken Cooper on an educational trip.

"Babe?" Erik asked again.

She felt more than saw Beau stiffen at the word *babe.* She turned to him, hoping that he could read her mind the way he'd seemed to do all weekend long. *This is my chance for a car,* she thought at him, begging him to follow her lead. *This is freedom, right here. I just have to go along with this one thing to get everything I want.*

But she couldn't see anything in his eyes. Not the slightest glimmer of understanding or anything else. Just that slight mocking gleam. Was he daring her? She couldn't tell.

So she did what she had to do. She turned back toward Erik and forced a smile.

"Yeah," she said. She turned the same smile on her parents. "The light show was cool. Really fun."

She heard her parents start talking again, but this time to Cooper. Erik pulled her closer with the arm that still felt strange around her. And then he leaned down and kissed her.

She had a flash of his lips on that girl in the Stanford dorm. Of his hands all over her body. She wondered—briefly and almost hysterically—just how many girls Erik had been kissing. If they all seemed interchangeable to him, and she was just one more.

But maybe that girl had been a onetime thing. Maybe he hadn't been lying the entire time he was away at school. Maybe he really did care for her—why else would he go to the trouble of saving her ass like this?

She didn't know the answer to any of these questions, so she kissed him back, quickly, and then eased away.

Erik was trying to catch her gaze, but Lila looked at Beau instead.

His face was frozen, arrested. He blinked, but not before Lila saw the hurt and confusion.

And anger.

She reached out for him before she remembered herself—before she remembered that Erik still had his beefy arm slung around her shoulders. She dropped her hand back to her side. Beau ignored her completely.

She winced, like she could actually hear what he was thinking. That she was exactly as superficial and vain as he'd accused her of being, and he'd been crazy to think otherwise. That she cared more about herself—and that car—than she did about anything or anyone else, including her own brother and especially including him. That she deserved a guy like Erik. That she disgusted him, and the best thing she'd ever done in her life was leave him the first time. She felt a sob build inside her chest, but she couldn't let it out. She swallowed it down.

"I think we'd better get going," Beau said politely. Too politely. He beckoned Tyler over and rested his hand on his brother's shoulder. Then he nodded at Lila's parents. He very carefully did not look at Lila or Erik. "Merry Christmas, everyone."

"You too," Lila's mother replied.

"E-mail me as soon as Santa comes," Cooper said to Tyler, very seriously. "We have to compare notes."

"Totally," Tyler agreed in the same tone.

And then Beau grabbed Tyler's hand, turned, and was gone.

20

Christmas morning smelled like pine, coffee, and her mother's world-famous cinnamon buns. Lila followed the buttery scent down from her bedroom, happy to pad around in her socks and Gap Body pajama bottoms, not caring how she looked. She'd spent about an hour in the shower the night before, washing away every last remnant of the weekend. Good-bye, strange moments with Beau. Good-bye, Beau's kisses. Good-bye, California freeways and Seattle snow and Beau's hand cupping her cheek so gently, like he was still in love with her the way he used to be.

Good-bye.

Lila walked into the family room and managed a smile. Santa had made his appearance sometime after the Beckwiths had finished decorating their tree the night before. Lila had sent Erik away, telling him she'd call him after she'd processed his apologies. She knew that he found the whole Christmas Eve decoration thing bizarre anyway, since *his* mother insisted on having *their* tree up and decorated almost before the Thanksgiving dishes were cleared.

But Lila liked the Beckwith tradition. The whole family settled in on Christmas Eve and went through the boxes of ornaments together. Lila showed everyone the Christmas card she'd been working on, and her dad sang along to Christmas carols in that funny, deep voice he used that always made Lila and her mother giggle. Cooper worked himself into a frenzy of anticipation that was not helped by too much hot cocoa with marshmallows, or the traditional Christmas chili that Mrs. Beckwith put on the stove.

Lila padded into the kitchen and smiled at her mother.

"Merry Christmas!" her mother said.

"You too," Lila said, going over and giving her mother a kiss on the cheek. "I've been waiting all year for these cinnamon rolls, Mom."

"Me too," Mrs. Beckwith confessed, and they shared a moment of perfect, cinnamon-y communion with cream cheese frosting on top.

Lila sighed happily.

And then realized that it was way too quiet.

"Where's our little Christmas elf?" she asked, a nervous quiver in her voice.

Had he taken off again? How long had it been since she'd seen him last night? She automatically glanced at her watch—then remembered that she'd taken it off last night and left it in a jumble on her bedside table. Cooper could be anywhere. . . .

"Your father took Cooper on a walk," Mrs. Beckwith said, breaking into Lila's private freak-out session. Lila drew a deep breath. "He woke up at six and refused to go back to bed. He was bouncing off the walls."

Lila squinted across the room, picking up the time from the clock on the stove. Nine fifteen. "I can't believe he let me sleep this long," she said after taking a huge swig of her coffee.

"Merry Christmas," her mother said again, with a meaningful look.

Lila laughed and settled into her favorite chair at the kitchen table, pulling her feet up under her. After the weekend she'd had, she should have slept all day. But something at the edge of her mind wouldn't let her relax. She held her coffee mug between her hands and scowled into it while her mother bustled around, frying bacon in her cast iron skillet. It was the perfect complement to Christmas morning cinnamon buns, but Lila's head was still stuck on the night before.

All she kept asking herself—while he was telling her how sorry he was, but couldn't quite repress the hint of that cocky grin that had always made her melt before—was why she had liked him in the first place. Was it just that Erik was so different, in every possible way, from Beau? Or was Beau right about why she'd gone with Erik three years ago—because it was easier? Because Erik was a relief after stormy, intimate, troubled Beau?

And why, after he'd said all those *horrible* things to her, couldn't she stop thinking about Beau Hodges?

Lila jerked back to the present when the front door slammed, and Cooper came racing into the house at top speed and top volume.

"Here we go," Lila said to her mother as Cooper careened into the kitchen. But she was laughing.

"Lila!" he cried. His eyes were wild with excitement and he wore a red T-shirt that was just as stained as his green one had been. "Finally! Did you *see*? I stayed up all night and I still didn't hear him, but he came! Did you look?"

Lila opened her mouth to deliver the usual put-down, but stopped herself. She looked at her tiny, enthusiastic little brother. What was wrong with being excited about things? Christmas only came once a year. And the truth was, there was something in Lila that missed believing in Christmas the way Cooper did. Maybe Christmas was the one time all year everyone got to pretend they were still kids. The one time they got to believe that magic still happened. Lila let him grab her by the arm and propel her out into the family room.

"Check it out!" Cooper cried. He flung out one of his arms, as if presenting the scene. Holly was hung over the mantel, and the Beckwiths' newly decorated tree sat in the corner, beneath it an array of shiny wrapped gifts, sparkling with promise.

"I don't know why you're so excited," Lila teased him, even though the sight of the tree gave her a little jolt of excitement too. "I bet none of those are for you anyway."

"The global warming can't be too bad if he came anyway, can it?" Cooper asked then, in an urgent whisper, frowning up at her. His brown eyes held all the worries and concerns of an adult. "I mean, it has to be okay, right?"

Lila paused. Had she really wanted to disabuse him of this notion only a few days ago? "He's Santa Claus, Cooper," she said gently. "He can handle anything."

"All right," Mr. Beckwith said, walking into the room. He held the tray of cinnamon buns and bacon before him, partially covering up his *Han Shot First* T-shirt. "Let the wild rumpus begin!"

Lila settled into the morning, swigging coffee and enjoying herself more than she could remember in a long time. Her father made a silly hat from all the leftover ribbons and wore it proudly. Her mother flushed with pleasure over the gifts she got, carefully saving all the wrapping paper and reading the cards out loud. But Cooper was the one having the most fun. He was like a puppy on a sugar high, with more energy than Lila could imagine ever having in her life, running around the room dispensing presents like his goal was to be an honorary elf. It probably was.

Lila tore through her gifts with pleasure, losing herself in the rip of wrapping paper and the crinkle of the leftover pieces. She ooohed over the delicate gold necklace that Erik had left beneath the tree, and solemnly thanked Cooper for the ceramic elephant he'd clearly slaved over before giving it to her.

"I know you like turtles more than elephants," Cooper said, as if this had been a topic of intense debate. Lila couldn't remember ever having stated a preference for either turtles or elephants. Or really having mentioned them, for that matter. "But I really wanted to make an elephant, so . . ."

"Turtles are cool," she said, hefting the surprisingly heavy elephant into the air. Cooper watched her, like he was trying to read her mind. Lila gazed at the creature, glazed to a high shine and painted bright red and green. "But," she continued, meeting Cooper's concerned gaze, "I think a Christmas elephant is pretty awesome."

Cooper sagged in relief, and Lila bent over and gave him a noisy kiss on the cheek. As she straightened, she caught the satisfied look her parents passed between them.

Lila glanced around the room, at the couch she'd spent so many evenings lounging and doing homework on, at the snow globes her mother collected, at the family Christmas cards from years past, sitting proudly on the mantel. For the first time it really hit her that she wouldn't be living with her three nutty family members after the summer. She would be one of those people she'd seen crowded into the hallway in Erik's dorm at Stanford. She'd be sleeping in those uncomfortable dorm beds and sharing a communal shower. No more annoying Cooper monologues about ridiculous things over the dinner table. No more of her dad singing, or her mother's high-pitched giggle that made her sound like a little girl.

And after college, there would be life—or so all her teachers warned her. *Life*, which meant living somewhere glamorous, Lila hoped, and *glamorous* definitely didn't involve this house or these people. Soon enough, she would *only* see them at times like this. She had the sense that life was suddenly moving really, really fast. That she should stop and catch her breath before it was too late. She coughed to hide the sudden choked-up feeling in her throat.

"I'll take the empty mugs to the kitchen," she announced, standing up. "Unless anyone wants more coffee?"

"Wait!" Cooper cried. He got up from the floor and crossed to the tree. "What about this last one?"

He pulled a small, oddly shaped little package from where it had been hanging from a ribbon on the tree. Lila frowned down at it when he pressed it into her hands. It was very light, but definitely not one of the gift certificates that her parents sometimes liked to hang from the tree on Christmas morning.

Mystified, she ripped open the wrapping paper. And then stared at the object that spilled into her hand.

It was a key.

More specifically, a car key.

Lila gaped at it, her mind reeling. Could it be? Could it possibly . . . ?

She looked up, dazed, to see her parents grinning at her.

"Why don't you take a look outside," her father suggested.

"Oh my God," Lila breathed. For a moment, she couldn't move. "Oh my *God*," she said again, and shot to her feet. She hurled herself toward the back door, and scrambled across the patio and into the driveway . . .

. . . where what to her wondering eyes did appear, but a glossy black convertible VW Beetle with a red ribbon on the hood. It was her dream car. It was sitting in her driveway. And she was gripping the key in her fist.

"You guys . . . ," she whispered in disbelief. She moved closer to the car and ran her fingers along the glossy hood. It felt like satin. Satin that could take you anywhere you wanted to go. "I can't believe this!"

"We were planning to give you a car for your birthday in January," Mr. Beckwith said, standing in the driveway, a cascade of ribbons tied haphazardly all over his head. The decoration looked even sillier out in the morning sun, but Lila didn't even think to tell him to take it off. "But we wanted to surprise you, and we knew you were expecting the car on your birthday, so we decided to bring it home for Christmas instead."

"This is amazing!" Lila cried. She went and gave her dad a big hug. "Is that where you guys were? Picking up this car? I thought you were visiting Aunt Lucy in Phoenix."

"We were doing both," Mrs. Beckwith said, looking pleased. She hugged Lila tight when Lila turned to her. "I know we've been riding you pretty hard this year, but we wanted to make sure you were ready. A car is a big responsibility. And so is college. You have a big year ahead of you, sweetheart."

Lila felt her world shift a little bit as her parents' words sank in. Maybe the fact that they expected her to be tougher and stronger meant that she *was* tougher and stronger. It was a new, unfamiliar truth that was hard to get her head around. She felt heat at the back of her eyes, and knew she was about to cry.

"I love you guys," Lila said into her mother's neck, and then threw out her arm to include her dad, too. "Thank you so, so, *so* much!"

They all laughed when Cooper collided with their legs, wanting in on the Beckwith group hug moment.

It was the perfect Christmas morning. It was warm and sunny, and the light bounced off of the gorgeous Beetle and made a rainbow on the driveway. Lila carefully opened the driver's door and then eased inside, inhaling the sharp new-car scent. She waved at her parents through the windshield and told herself that nothing would ever be as great as this moment.

She had everything she ever wanted.

And yet somehow, for some reason, she wasn't as happy as she thought she'd be.

21

HOLLANDER HOUSE
LOS ANGELES
DECEMBER 25
9:20 P.M.

Lila's new car was all anyone could talk about later that night, when Lila and her friends crowded into the family room at the Hollanders' house. It was their group's Christmas tradition to hang out long after everyone had put in their required family time— or, for those not celebrating Christmas, Chinese food and movie time. The Hollander house was always the best choice, because everyone gravitated to Erik and Carly, of course, but also because Mr. and Mrs. Hollander believed in looking the other way, rather than having the kids go out and drink somewhere else.

"We are going to spend serious time on the Pacific Coast Highway in that baby," Carly declared, hugging Lila as they stood in the kitchen, leaning up against the center island while the usual North Valley High shenanigans went on all around them.

"Yeah, we are," Lila said at once, smiling—but she didn't feel the tug of Carly's smile the way she usually did. It was like she was distanced, somehow, from the low-key party going on all around her.

Carly's smile faded a little, and her expression turned quizzical. "Why aren't you, like, dancing with joy? Don't you think you can dance?" she asked, only half-teasing, but clearly trying to make Lila laugh with the reference to their favorite reality show.

"Sugar coma," Lila said, rubbing her belly. It was a handy excuse for her weird mood. "I can't believe how many Christmas cookies I ate today. I seriously could not be stopped."

"Oh my God, Lila!" Yoon appeared at her elbow, Rebecca close behind her. They both looked delighted to see Lila, which made her feel . . . exhausted, somehow. All her interactions with them felt so forced. Had it always taken this much effort to hang out with her friends? "We missed you on Friday! But if that cute car is your prize for bailing, I totally get it."

Lila stuck her hands in the pockets of her jeans and realized that she'd actually forgotten all about her party. Even now, she couldn't really understand why she'd cared so much. What was the big deal with one more party? All of the same people were standing around in the Hollanders' kitchen right now, and nothing amazing had happened yet. Nothing ever did. It only sounded amazing later, when they all talked about it and made sure to leave other people out.

Good lord, she was starting to sound like Beau. What was next? Would she grow her hair out and try to look like a shaggy dog? She shook her head, as if to chase thoughts of Beau away, and looked up at her friends.

"I didn't bail so much as get grounded," Lila pointed out mildly. She smiled anyway. "Was it fun?"

"It rocked," Rebecca said immediately. Yoon looked pleased.

"It was fine," Carly said dismissively, twirling a strand of her blond curls around her finger. She looked away, and Lila did too, wondering what Carly saw when she looked at her house. The open-plan kitchen blending into the family room, every corner stuffed full of Christmas paraphernalia. Red and green to the gills, and North Valley High's most popular kids—past and present—hanging out in little groups, laughing and talking.

"Whatever," Carly said. She turned to Lila. "Where do you think we should go on our first road trip? Mexico?"

"Ooh," Yoon said, as if she'd never in her life wanted to do anything more. Lila could actually see Yoon switch gears. She could *hear* the calculation: *Forget about the party, Carly's all about the car.* "I want to hit Cabo. How awesome would that be?"

"I love Cabo!" Rebecca cried, performing the same social gymnastics.

Lila fell quiet, because Erik was coming over then. He broke away from his posse of ex–football friends, who were congregating together closer to the French doors that led out to the pool, swapping tales of their college exploits and the exams they all claimed they'd failed from being too hungover.

Naturally, all of Lila's friends watched his approach. Carly leaned against Lila and smiled broadly at her brother. Yoon flipped her glossy hair over her shoulders and arched her back. Rebecca fluffed up her own chestnut pixie cut and then squinted her green eyes in frank, obvious appraisal. The funny thing was, they didn't even know what had happened. Lila hadn't mentioned Erik's kissing exploits to a single soul—because how would that make her look? The cheated-on, foolish, high school girlfriend—as big a loser as she'd been once upon a time? So her friends were seeing Erik Hollander, God of North Valley High, as he came over to play the perfect boyfriend.

"Hey, babe," he said casually, his hazel eyes warm on Lila's. As if he didn't notice the way Yoon and Rebecca hung on his every syllable. But Lila knew that he did. He probably thrived on it, the way she once had. "Do you want a drink?"

Lila twirled the bottle of Corona she held in her hand and shrugged. "No," she said. "I'm good."

Erik smiled and leaned in to press a kiss to Lila's temple. She caught the envious look that Rebecca and Yoon shot between them, and farther back, Jeannine Fargo let out a jealous sigh. Every girl in the room but Carly wanted to be Lila right then.

"I'm sorry," Erik whispered, so only Lila could hear. She smiled at him again, not wanting to get into another round of excuses and explanations. Hadn't she told him it was fine? He'd met her at the door tonight, brimming with new apologies. But Lila didn't want to think about it anymore. She just wanted to move on. Start fresh. Maybe try to get to know Erik all over again—this time, with her eyes wide open.

But the more he talked about how sorry he was, the more she had to think about *why* he was sorry, which led to picturing him with that girl. And every time she looked at him, she pictured Beau punching him in the face. Erik had the now purple and blue shiner, which she'd heard him tell one of his friends was from a pickup game of touch football. *Right.* Just like he'd told his Stanford friends he needed a ride to L.A. because his car was in the shop.

"You guys are so cute," Rebecca said when Erik moved away, her green eyes alight like Erik Hollander was her own personal Christmas tree. She sighed. "It just gives me hope. That you guys are still together, I mean."

"It's better than a movie," Yoon agreed, sounding almost completely sincere this time. She held her hands over her heart, dramatically. "The way he looks at you!"

Lila glanced from Rebecca to Yoon to Carly. Even Carly

was smiling at her, ready to hear Lila affirm her supposed great romance with Erik. They were all waiting for Lila to say exactly what they wanted to hear: Yes, she was the luckiest girl in the world. Yes, they made their relationship work long-distance. Yes, dating Erik Hollander was everything it was cracked up to be, everything she'd ever aspired to in her life. They wanted to hear her affirm that their myths of popularity were true. Lila knew in that moment that her position as coqueen of North Valley High was solid. She knew that three days ago she would have reveled in this moment. It would have proven that she was exactly who and what she wanted to be: Lila Beckwith, social success.

But instead of the rush of triumph she'd expected to feel, she felt hollow inside. Instead of a big victory, she felt like she'd actually lost something.

Maybe it was the fact that Erik wasn't the perfect boyfriend— and maybe he hadn't ever been. Or maybe it was her sneaking suspicion that she'd had more fun singing that stupid "Roses Are Red" song with Beau than she'd had in a long time with these people.

Or maybe she was simply coming down with something. That might explain her stuffy head and the way she just wanted to sink down onto Carly's kitchen floor and cry.

"I'm a lucky girl," she said finally, because she had to say something. She put her mostly full Corona back down behind her on the counter. "I'll be right back," she whispered to Carly, and eased herself through the group toward the Hollanders' guest bathroom.

She took her time, and when she opened the door again, the sound of everyone laughing and talking seemed overwhelming. So instead of heading back into the party, Lila let herself out the side door and stood for a moment on the little back porch. The air was cold, and she could see stars overhead. She couldn't quite see her breath when she let it out, though she tried a few times.

And then Lila had to accept the fact that everything felt wrong. *She* felt wrong. She didn't even know why. Part of her wanted to take off screaming down the Hollanders' street, just to make noise and see what might happen. Another part of her wanted to go back inside and yell at all of her friends for being so . . . so . . . for being the way they were. So concerned with the same boring stuff, party after party, day after day, even after they went off to college.

Her hand rose to her temple and found the place where Erik had kissed her. She didn't exactly wipe the kiss away, but she thought about it.

Aside from the kiss in her family room, she hadn't kissed him at all since she'd gotten back. And . . . she didn't think she was suddenly going to wake up and want to start kissing him any time soon.

How could so much change so fast? Part of it was seeing him at Stanford—seeing what he was like when he thought she wasn't around. Lila wasn't an idiot. Erik hadn't been acting like someone with a guilty conscience. He hadn't even been hiding in some corner with that chick—he'd been standing there for everyone to see. That didn't strike her as the kind of thing someone would do if they were really that concerned about the girlfriend they'd left behind. It wasn't the kind of thing you did when you'd told your college friends you even *had* a girlfriend.

But the other part of it, Lila knew, was her. Spending all that time with Beau had reminded her of things she had tried really, really hard to forget. Not just Beau himself, which she didn't really want to think about, but the way they'd talked to each other. The feeling that she could say absolutely anything to him and he'd handle it. It might hurt his feelings, or he might disagree, but she didn't have to be careful with him like that.

It wasn't like that with Erik. When Lila had first started dating him, she'd been so starry-eyed. So determined to be the perfect girlfriend, the perfect best friend. What she'd ended up being instead was quiet. Submissive. Erik knew he would be forgiven anything. What was that thing her mother always said? That it was easier to ask for forgiveness than permission?

The stars up above her seemed farther away, and the wind picked up, rattling through the palm trees and sneaking beneath Lila's sweater to chill her skin. She thought about the whole stretch of her relationship with Erik, and had the uncomfortable feeling that Beau had been absolutely right to call her shallow. Wasn't she? Did she like Erik, or did she like the fact that everyone else—including her parents—liked Erik? Was she upset that he had cheated on her because she had trusted him, or because she was worried that it would get out and everyone would know she'd been made to look a fool? Was Erik Hollander anything more than a status symbol to her?

She didn't actually know.

But she did know that she would rather be grounded, her new car taken away, than *pretend* any longer. He could tell her parents what had really happened this weekend. She didn't care.

Filled with resolve, Lila turned and walked back inside.

"Where'd you go?" Erik asked, coming right over to her. She wondered, briefly, what he got out of this whole thing. Did he just like having people remember him at North Valley High? Was that why he bothered? Or was it just *easier* to keep a girl-friend back home than to break up with her? Why not have the comfort of Lila at home and the freedom to do whatever you pleased at college? If you didn't have a conscience, it would be easy.

"I'm sorry," she said quietly. She lifted up her hands, then let them drop. "But I don't think I can do this."

"What?" His voice wasn't quiet. He was probably too shocked

to keep it down. "What do you mean? Is this because of what happened at Stanford?"

Lila stiffened as everyone in the kitchen fell quiet and turned. No one even pretended not to stare.

"No," she said, looking Erik straight in the eyes. "Maybe. I don't know."

"Lila . . ." Erik searched her face, and what he saw there must have surprised him, because he took a step back. "You're breaking up with me?"

Lila almost winced. She hated the way he'd said that—like it was particularly unbelievable that *she* was breaking up with *him*. She snuck a look at the assembled crowd and gulped. Yoon and Rebecca were whispering to each other, their hands over their mouths and their eyes far too bright. Carly looked pale. Jeannine Fargo was chewing on a carrot stick, her head cocked to the side like she was watching television. Erik's friends were smirking and muttering to one another. She had the sudden urge to run away. But she didn't.

Lila straightened her spine, and met his gaze. "Yes," she said, the word heavy on her tongue, knowing that she was probably throwing away all the hard work of the last three years of her life. Knowing that with those three letters, she was sealing her North Valley High fate. The crowd gasped. "I am."

The next few minutes were blurry. Erik stormed out, while Lila's friends were visibly torn between going after still popular, now single Erik, or getting more dirt from Lila. She felt dazed. But that passed when Carly pulled her away from the group that had converged on Lila, into the darkened living room. Lila expected a hug and some words of comfort, which, frankly, she could use right now. Until she saw the scowl on Carly's face.

"What did you just do?" her supposed best friend asked her in an angry voice.

"I had to," Lila said, and shrugged helplessly.

Carly laughed slightly, an edge to her voice. "Are you crazy?" she demanded. "He's not going to take you back after you humiliated him in front of all of his friends, Lila. You get that, right?"

"I'm not the one who was cheating!" Lila threw at her. She hadn't wanted to out Erik, but he deserved it. And she knew Carly would be discreet.

She expected her friend to gasp, to express some kind of shock that perfect, beloved Erik could have done such a thing. But the other girl's glossy lips pressed together in a thin, hard line. She looked disgusted.

"Grow up, Lila," she said coldly. "What did you think would happen while he was away?"

Lila stared at her blond, beautiful best friend, stunned. It was like some alien had taken over Carly's body. She had no idea who Carly was right now.

Had she ever?

"This is about that loser ex-boyfriend of yours, isn't it?" Carly asked, her voice dropping low. "Erik told me you spent the weekend with him. I thought he was kidding." Her mouth twisted. "You really want to go back to the dark ages with that freak?"

Lila actually felt dizzy. She reminded herself that Carly was Erik's sister. She was bound to take his side. Even if it hurt Lila almost more than seeing Erik with that other girl had.

The only question was, why was Lila still standing there, taking it?

"See you around," she said. She had the sudden urge to laugh out loud. Because she was free, even if it hurt.

"Lila . . . ," Carly whispered, the expression on her pretty face changing from anger to confusion.

But Lila turned on her heel and let herself out the door. She knew as it slammed shut behind her that she had just committed complete and total North Valley High social suicide.

Apparently, hell *had* frozen over.

22

It had to be almost three in the morning, but Lila couldn't sleep.

She shifted around in her bed and then finally gave up. She swung her feet to the ground and sat there in the dark of her bedroom for a moment. She sighed.

Her room was done in blues and the occasional violet, like the flowers on her comforter. She sank her toes into the deep carpet and looked around. There was the Robert Pattinson poster on the wall near her desk, because *Twilight* or no *Twilight*, the guy was hot. And when he sang, he sounded like Ray LaMontagne. In the far corner, her old guitar was propped up against the wall, collecting dust and providing a little stand for the collection of hats that she never wore. Her closet door was open, her clothes tumbling out and across the floor in a riot of colors, twisted around boots and shoes and her school bag. She rubbed her hands over her face.

Her head was spinning, making her dizzy and feel something like panicked, but she couldn't seem to pick out any particular train of thought.

Liar.

She smirked at herself in the late-night—or was it early-morning?—gloom. She didn't *want* to pick out any specific line of thought, because she was giving herself insomnia in an effort to keep from thinking about one particular thing.

Beau.

Which wasn't really working. But the truth was, Lila had no idea what to do about it. About *him.* Even if she could get past the way he'd looked at her before leaving her with Erik, there was the small matter of all the things he'd said to her in the car. Some of which she was not exactly thrilled to admit were probably true.

Lila sighed again and stood up, then tiptoed her way downstairs. The house was quiet all around her, with the faintest sound of her father's snores from behind her parents' door. She poured herself a glass of milk and took a big, soothing gulp.

She wandered aimlessly across the kitchen floor, her bare feet feeling the chill of the linoleum. She looked into the family room and saw that the family computer was still on and flashing

that silly *Avengers* screen saver that Cooper liked. She went over
to turn it off.

She moved the mouse with her hand and blinked as the
screen saver gave way to Cooper's e-mail account, still open,
with his inbox up on the screen. Of course Cooper had run off
and left the computer running, despite the numerous times he'd
been told not to. Lila thought, with a smile, that it was going to
be pretty interesting around the Beckwith house when she was
off at college, and the true culprit would have to be addressed,
finally. She was surprised at the surge of affection she felt for all
of them, then. She was beginning to suspect she would miss her
whole family more than she'd ever imagined possible.

Lila went to shut Cooper's e-mail program down. But her
eye was caught by the most recent incoming email displayed in
his inbox, sent from Santa_Claus@northpole.com.

Lila laughed out loud. She debated for about three seconds,
and then clicked the message open. If he'd really wanted privacy, he should have closed down his e-mail account.

Dear Cooper,

*While you are always in the "Nice" column, Mrs. Claus
and I wanted to send you a special thank-you this year. We're
both grateful that you and Tyler were prepared to come all
the way up here to check on us. Not many people would be
brave enough to take a trip like that all by themselves!*

Global warming is scary, but it doesn't affect us as much as you might think. The weather here at the North Pole is always a little bit colder than you might see reported on the news. That's because the elves work hard to keep it that way. But we can't let CNN know about some of the elvish technologies we use, because, well, that's our little secret. So this will have to stay between you and me, but I wanted you to know: You have nothing to worry about.

The Mrs. tells me that the reindeer are all back and ready for the annual "End of Christmas" party that we throw to celebrate another great year of presents delivered to nice kids like you.

Yours,

S. Claus

P.S. Thanks for the cookies and milk.

It was the sweetest e-mail Lila had ever read, and she knew exactly who had sent it to Cooper.

Beau.

And suddenly, she knew what she had to do.

23

Lila picked her way through Beau's backyard, weaving around the landscaped holly bushes with their sharp leaves and under the big oak tree toward his window. Thank God his room was at the back of the house, unlike his mother's or brother's.

The neighborhood was quiet all around her. All the houses were dark and locked up tight against lunatics wandering around in the night. Palm trees moved high above her, and there wasn't even a dog barking somewhere to break the silence.

She bit her lip for a moment, hesitating. She could just sneak back to her car and drive away, and no one would ever be the wiser. After all, it was after three in the morning. The night was dark and very clear, and cold, though not as cold as it had been way up north. She didn't even shiver as she stood there outside Beau's window.

She was about to do something she could only categorize as crazy. But it was something she knew she had to do.

Lila hoisted up the guitar she'd brought with her. She'd excavated it from under a collection of baseball caps and ugly berets and a western cowboy hat she was sure she'd never laid eyes on before. She'd tuned it in the car, wincing at how out of practice she was, and how clumsy and *wrong* her hands felt on the guitar she'd once viewed as an extension of herself.

And now here she was. One hundred percent ready.

Well. Maybe more like 75 percent ready.

Lila decided there was no time like the present. It was only going to get colder, and then the sun would come up, and this definitely wasn't the kind of thing she wanted to do in daylight.

She started playing, making a mess of the chords. Her hands protested moves that had once been second nature to her. Her mind knew what to do, but somehow she couldn't quite get her fingers to do it. It made her feel even more foolish than she already did. Like it wasn't bad enough that she was outside Beau's window in the middle of the night having a vintage *Say Anything* moment—did she also have to suck at playing the guitar while she did it?

But she had no time to think about that, because she'd played the opening chords twice, and now it was time to sing.

She had never truly forgotten the words of their little song, but she'd had no choice but to remember them this weekend. She'd already sung them once—so what was one more time?

Of course, Lila thought as she opened her mouth and began to sing, it was a lot easier to sing a song when you didn't have to sing it alone. When your soprano could be tangled up in and supported by Beau's scratchy, sexy tenor. Alone, her voice seemed to wobble in the night air. The guitar still sounded off—but maybe that was just her playing. Or the fact that it was after 3 a.m. and normal people were all tucked up in bed, with visions of sugarplums and new holiday memories in their dreams.

Lila sang.

"Roses are red and violets are blue, daisies are yell—achoo! Achoo!" she sang. *"Claritin helps me through the night—allergy meds make love all right."*

She kept singing even though she knew it sounded less than stellar. She sang because for once, she didn't care what she looked like or what she sounded like or whether it was cool. She sang because it was the only song she could sing. And because it was the only way she could think of to tell Beau everything that she needed to tell him, in a way that only he would understand, and that he couldn't possibly misunderstand.

But when the song was finished, and the last note had faded away, Beau's window was still dark. No light came on inside. The palm trees rustled in the breeze, and Lila was suddenly all too aware that it was very late, and cold, and she was standing all alone in her ex-boyfriend's backyard. Some people might call that kind of thing *stalking*.

For a minute she thought that maybe she should play something else—but she almost immediately thought better of it. She didn't want to wake up the neighbors. The very thought of having to explain her presence this late on Christmas, clutching a guitar and singing loudly in the wee hours of the morning . . .

She turned away and headed back for her car. Her beautiful, glorious new car, that she was happy to have, of course, but didn't seem to solve anything the way she'd expected it would. She hadn't considered the fact that having her own space just meant that she had more time to sit alone and reflect on all the things she should have done differently. Like, say, the last few years of her life.

Lila walked to her car and opened the back door, putting her guitar back in its dusty case. She felt worse than she had in a long time—much worse, in fact, than she had after she caught Erik cheating. Worse than when Carly had turned into a stranger in front of her.

She'd lost Beau. And she hadn't even been smart enough to hold on to him when she'd gotten him back so unexpectedly, so briefly. And with him, she knew, she'd lost a part of herself.

Maybe forever.

Lila put her hand on the Beetle's door, ready to sink inside and give in to the feelings, give in to the sadness, give in to the tears.

And then she felt a hand on her arm.

All of her breath left her in a rush, and something hopeful sparked inside of her. She slowly turned around.

Beau stood there, his blue and white striped pajama bottoms rumpled and his shaggy dark hair even more of a mess than usual. His blue eyes were sleepy—but shining.

"Nice car," he said, sounding gruff. But there was a hint of a smile at the corner of his mouth.

Lila blinked at him. He looked half-asleep and scruffy and more beautiful than she could really take in.

"Want to take a ride?" she said, her voice sounding stronger than she felt. Her heart was knocking hard against her ribs. What did Beau coming out here mean? Had he heard her song? Had he forgiven her? Or had he just come out to tell her to quiet down?

Beau's hand felt warm on her skin. A corner of his lips twitched.

"Like maybe to San Jose?" He smiled wider. "I think I left my car there."

Lila smiled back, taking in his tousled hair, bare feet, another ancient concert T-shirt. She could have stared at him forever.

"So . . . ," Beau said after a moment. His other hand came up to take Lila's free arm, pulling her close. Tiny shivers rushed up and down her spine. "Did I hear somebody singing our song out here, or was I just tripping after too much Christmas ham?"

Lila shrugged, but she smiled. Being so close to him felt precarious and glorious, and she was afraid to breathe, afraid that anything she might do might break the spell between them.

"I don't know," she said, tilting up her chin, marveling once again at how well they fit together. How easy it was to stand like this, so close—matched. It felt like Lila was finally where she belonged.

"How about an encore?" Beau asked, his voice nearly a whisper.

And then he kissed her. And she kissed him back.

Not for the first time.

And definitely not for the last.

Wouldn't you *kill* to see Private come to life?

 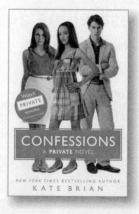

Catch the exclusive Web series of the first four Private novels!

Some girls would die
for a life of Privilege . . .
Some would even kill for it.

Don't miss a minute of this
delectably naughty series by
bestselling author Kate Brian.

Now available

Now available

Available
October 2009